REBELS
OF THE
LAMP

REBELS OF THE LAMP

BY
MICHAEL M.B. GALVIN
& PETER SPEAKMAN

DISNEP • HYPERION

LOS ANGELES   NEW YORK

Printed in the United States of America
First Edition, May 2015
1 3 5 7 9 10 8 6 4 2
G475-5664-5-15046

Library of Congress Cataloging-in-Publication Data

Galvin, Michael M.B., author.
 Rebels of the lamp/Michael M.B. Galvin, Peter Speakman.—First edition.
  pages cm.—(The Jinn Wars)
 Summary: "Parker Quarry is only twelve years old, and he's about to enter a war that has been brewing for centuries. When his mother sends him to New Hampshire to stay with his cousin Theo, Parker expects to be bored out of his mind. But then he stumbles across an ancient container—with a real genie inside—and life for Parker gets way more exciting. But there are those who seek to unleash the devastating power of the genies onto the world, and he may be humanity's only hope at surviving."—Provided by publisher.
 ISBN 978-1-4231-7957-3
 [1. Genies—Fiction. 2. Magic—Fiction. 3. War—Fiction.] I. Speakman, Peter, author. II. Title.
 PZ7.1.G35Re 2015
 [Fic]—dc23   2014029969

Visit www.DisneyBooks.com

ACKNOWLEDGMENTS

Thanks to Eddie Gamarra, Eric Robinson, Jeremy Bell, and Peter McHugh of the Gotham Group, Valerie Phillips and Trevor Astbury at Paradigm, Jim Garavente, Russell Hollander, Faye Atchison, all the friends and family members that put up with us while we're writing, and everybody at Disney • Hyperion, especially our patient and tireless editors Kevin Lewis and Ricardo Mejías.

For Laura, Devon, and Zachary: the best adventurers for the biggest adventures.
—P.S.

For Chelsea, of course.
—M.M.B.G.

PROLOGUE

PARKER QUARRY HAD NEVER DRIVEN a car a hundred and fifty miles an hour before.

Actually, if you want to get all technical about it, Parker had never driven a car at all before. Not even once. Not even in a parking lot. They don't let you drive cars when you're twelve years old. He had checked.

He grinned. This was, without a doubt, by almost anybody's definition, cool.

"Dog!"

Parker heard Reese scream out, but he had already seen the dog in the middle of the road. He had spotted him almost a mile away. What was it, exactly? A Boston terrier? Some kind of a retriever? A labradoodle? It was hard to say. All of Parker's senses seemed sharper, but he wasn't really a dog person.

"Parker!"

"I heard you, Reese. Sheesh," Parker said.

It would have been impossible for him not to hear her. Reese was wedged into the backseat of the red Porsche 911 Turbo S, and her head was only three inches from Parker's ear. It was a backseat designed more for small children or groceries than actual people. Reese wouldn't have been comfortable back there even if she was alone, and she wasn't. Parker's cousin, Theo, was crammed back there, too, one hand gripping the side of the car so hard his knuckles were turning white, and one hand held up to his mouth in case he got any sicker than he already was.

The backseat was not suitable for two junior-high kids. It would be perfect for, say, a Boston terrier, or some kind of a retriever, or a labradoodle.

Like the one that the car was hurtling toward.

"Parker!"

Parker thought that Reese might actually have a heart attack. With all the skill of an F1 driver, he downshifted the Porsche and turned the wheel, missing the mystery mutt by a good foot and a half. The dog was safe to resume his life of barking happily at skateboarders and urinating on things that needed to be urinated on.

The Porsche growled as Parker stabbed the gas again and continued his automotive assault on the winding, tree-lined back roads of Cahill, New Hampshire.

"I think I'm gonna throw up," said Theo.

"Deep breaths, buddy," Parker said. "In through your nose and out through your mouth."

The man in the passenger seat sighed and crossed his arms against his broad chest. He feared that he would never get used to twelve-year-olds or cars. He was tall, with sharp features, and eyes that never seemed to decide what color they wanted to be. He was dressed in black robes. He might have been twenty or he might have been fifty. It was hard to say.

"Um, Parker?"

"Yes, Theo?"

Theo was too ill to get the words out, so he just pointed. A police car was turning onto the road behind them.

"Oh. Well, maybe they're not after us," Parker said.

The cop turned on his flashing lights and sirens and stomped on the gas, his rear tires erupting in smoke as he joined the chase.

"Huh. Well, that's not a problem."

Parker shifted again, and the sports car lurched forward as if someone had attached rockets to the back bumper.

"Five hundred and sixty horsepower," Parker bragged as the police car faded from his rearview mirror. "I don't think they're going to catch us."

"They don't have to catch us," said Reese. "They have radios."

She pointed. Three more police cars were parked sideways, blocking the road about a mile ahead. The cops were standing behind their cars, guns drawn. The officer in charge held up a bullhorn.

"This is the Cahill police. Stop your vehicle."

Reese turned pale. "I think he wants us to stop."

Parker just smiled.

"I mean it, Parker. I can't get in trouble with the police. My mom's expecting me to apply to Harvard in four years. My safety school is Stanford!"

"There's no way out," said the cop. "Stop the car. Now."

Parker frowned. On the one hand, it was a beautiful day and he was really enjoying the drive. On the other hand, policemen with badges and shotguns seemed to really, sincerely want him to stop the car.

It was a no-brainer.

"Guys," Parker said, "You might want to hang on to something."

Theo groaned. "I knew this was a bad idea. I just knew it."

Parker mashed the gas pedal. The Porsche accelerated like it was dropped out of a plane. It was headed straight at the roadblock.

"Are you ready, Fon-Rahm?" Parker asked.

The man in the passenger seat nodded.

"Then do your thing, please."

Wisps of smoke came from the man's eyes.

"I just knew it," said Theo.

The cops saw the car speeding toward them. The officer with the bullhorn shook his head. "I don't think that guy's going to stop," he said.

He was right, too. The Porsche was going to smash into the police cars. At a hundred and fifty miles an hour.

"Um, I'll be over there," said one of the officers, pointing toward the side of the road.

"Wait! Stay here!" said the top cop, but it was too late. Every one of his officers had abandoned the roadblock.

The officer in charge thought for a moment. Then he dropped the bullhorn and ran off the road to be with his buddies. His wife was making tacos for dinner, and he liked tacos, and he wouldn't be able to eat them if his teeth were scattered all over the highway.

The Porsche charged at the cop cars. This was going to be messy.

"Now!" said Parker.

Fon-Rahm lifted his left hand and waved it through the air, bored. Smoke rose from the ground, and bits of wood, sheets of metal, and street signs leaped up from the sides of the road and magically shaped themselves into a makeshift ramp.

The cops stared with dropped jaws as the Porsche hit the ramp and sailed over the police cars. It landed with a thud and a storm of sparks past the roadblock, and it didn't pause for a second before speeding off.

Reese scrunched up her face. "Well, at least we're not getting arrested," she said.

"Please, Parker, please stop the car," said Theo.

"I will in just a few minutes." Parker looked the man in black over. "I know we're the only ones who can see you, but those robes really give me the willies. How about changing into something a little more contemporary?"

A light mist filled the car. When it cleared, Fon-Rahm's robes were gone, replaced with a sleek black suit.

"Is this more to your liking?" he asked.

"Very sharp. The color fits your personality."

"You try my patience, boy. I am Fon-Rahm of the Jinn, not a dress-up toy."

Parker shook his head and clucked. "Fon-Rahm, I'm surprised at you. Have you not been wearing your seat belt this whole time? Put in on, please. Safety first."

Fon-Rahm put his seat belt on and continued sulking.

"And cheer up, Rommy, old pal. This is what us humans call fun."

Parker stepped on the accelerator and grinned. You know what was cool? Having your own personal genie.

That was cool.

1

TWO WEEKS EARLIER

THE GODS STARED DOWN FROM THE
ceiling.

Mercury blasted through space, wings flapping at his ankles.
Venus lounged on a cloud, her long, black hair flowing behind
her. Jupiter held lightning in his hands as if to warn humans not
to get too close. Atlas held up the world, weary but unbroken.
Imagine propping up the entire planet on your shoulders for all
eternity. It was a thankless job, but somebody had to do it.

Mr. Ardigo knew the feeling.

"All right, all right, settle down, please. Please. Please."

He had volunteered—no, he had *begged* to bring his class to the
Griffith Observatory. The place was, as the kids would say, sick.

It was equipped with massive telescopes and a planetarium, and it was set smack-dab on the edge of a cliff overlooking the entire city. The view was amazing. From the right angle you could even see the Hollywood sign. "It'll be educational!" he had said. "It'll broaden their horizons! It'll show them the grandeur of space and how small we are compared to the rest of the universe!"

If it showed them anything, though, it was that one teacher (okay, two, if you count Mrs. Haverkamp, but she was useless. A nice woman, sure, and great with computers, but when faced with screaming kids she was as handy as a Nerf hammer) could in no way hope to successfully wrangle forty seventh graders through a Los Angeles landmark. There were just too many of them. Mr. Ardigo was simply outmanned.

The kids were all standing around a circular hole in the floor of the marble rotunda, watching a pendulum swing from the center of the mural of the gods overhead. That was fine, he thought. The pendulum's swing was proof that the Earth was rotating, and that was a science lesson in itself. He wanted the kids to learn.

What he didn't want them to do was act like what they were: twelve-year-olds on a field trip. The boys shoved each other into walls while the girls kept up a regimen of near constant shrieking. What was there to scream about? The pendulum was neat, in a nerdy way, but really? The second these kids stepped out of school, they lost their minds. He thought they might burn off some of that extra energy on the bus ride over, but their supply seemed limitless.

Mr. Ardigo had a headache already. He checked his watch. They had been at the observatory less than fifteen minutes.

"The planetarium show starts in twenty-two minutes," he said over the roar. "And then everyone will get a chance to look through the telescope."

He checked his guidebook. "Apparently, we'll be looking at a very rare planetary alignment. The last time it happened was over three thousand years ago. Kendra!"

Kendra stopped leaning so far over the railing that she would absolutely fall in and looked at him blankly. A small, small victory. She did not stop shrieking, though. They never do, thought Mr. Ardigo.

"There's a lot to see in here, and I want to get to it all, but you're all going to have to cooperate, okay? Guys?"

Mr. Ardigo noticed that he was tapping his foot, and made a conscious effort to stop. He was always drumming his fingers or clicking a pen. Stuff like that drove his wife nuts. She was right. He was too nervous. He had to learn to relax. He also had to make more money. Mrs. Ardigo's dream was that her husband would ditch teaching altogether and open up a Quiznos.

He would never do it. He loved teaching. Well, not on this particular *day*, but in general, he loved teaching.

"Okay, let's go, let's go."

His class broke away from the pendulum in one noisy lump and rushed past him on their way into the exhibits.

"Stick together, please, and keep your hands to yourself," Mr. Ardigo said. "We're going to be quiet and we're going to be respectful. That goes double for you, Parker."

The teacher froze. He scanned the line of kids once, and then again. No Parker.

"Parker? Has anybody seen Parker?"

Nobody had. Mr. Ardigo let out a sigh and stared at the ceiling. Atlas, he thought. Atlas had it easy.

Parker twisted the puzzle again. It was a series of four interlocking metal squares, and the idea was to make them all line up. It should be easy, he thought, except for some reason, it was ridiculously hard. He would get two in the right place, and then one would be way out of whack, and then he would fix that one, and ruin all the work he had done before. The thing was impossible. Maybe if he could take the price tag off.

"I can never figure those things out," said a woman behind him.

She was about sixty years old, and she was wearing a blue shirt with a collar and a Griffith Observatory name tag that read JUNE.

Parker smiled sweetly at her. He was just an innocent kid browsing the racks of a gift store. There's nothing less suspicious than that.

"Me neither," he said, putting the puzzle back on the shelf with the astronaut ice cream and the Lunar Lander play set. "But, you see, it's not for me. I'm looking for a present. For my mother."

"Aren't you sweet! Is it her birthday?"

"No, she's . . ." His eyes found the floor. "She's in the hospital."

"Oh, I'm so sorry," said June. She was, too.

"Yeah, she's pretty sick. I thought maybe, since I was here, I could get her something to cheer her up. I got her some flowers and stuff but it's still pretty depressing in her room."

"Well, how about a stuffed animal? People love these!"

She held up a stuffed monkey wearing a NASA space suit.

"That's great! Really great! But I was thinking maybe something like that?"

Parker pointed to a crystal sculpture of a shooting star lodged at the top of the highest shelf in the store.

"Oh!" she said. "That is pretty."

June bit her bottom lip. She was a small woman, smaller than Parker, even, and he was twelve. If she was going to get that sculpture, it was going to take some effort.

"Let me just get that for you."

June stood on her toes and reached as high as she could.

As soon as her back was turned, Parker expertly grabbed the metal puzzle and slipped it into the pocket of his jacket.

June's fingers touched the sculpture. For a second it looked like it might fall, but June caught it and showed it triumphantly to Parker. "Ha! Got it!"

Parker looked at the light sparkling off the crystal.

"Is it okay if I come back for it later?" asked Parker. "That way I won't have to carry it around with me the rest of the day. I might break it. I'm pretty klutzy."

"Oh, you are not. I'll bet you're a natural athlete."

"Could you set it aside for me? Please?"

"Of course. You come back for it whenever you would like."

Parker thanked her and walked out the glass doors. It was that easy, he thought. If only he could get up the guts to grab some stuff out of a real store. Then maybe he wouldn't be the only kid he knew without a decent skateboard. Or a flat-screen TV. Or an iPhone.

He smiled a sly smile. Then he looked in the window of the

gift shop and saw June struggling to put the crystal star back on the shelf.

Parker sighed.

He walked back into the gift shop and steadied June while she put the thing back. Then she thanked him, and he sneaked the metal puzzle out of his pocket and back on the shelf. He never would have solved it, anyway.

Parker left the gift shop. He had better get back. Mr. Ardigo might have noticed he had left the group, and the last thing Parker needed, really, was to get in trouble again. His mom would kill him. Before he could take two steps, though, Parker was confronted by two of his classmates.

"Hey, Parker, what are you doing in the gift shop? You know you can't afford anything in there."

Great, Parker thought. Jason Sussman and his buddy Adam. They were two kids with more money than brains, and they were not fans of Parker. Both Jason and Adam were bigger than he was. In fact, almost every guy in his class was bigger than Parker. His mother told him he was going to hit a growth spurt soon, but Parker would believe it when he saw it.

"Jason. Adam. What's up?"

"Adam and I were just admiring your shoes," said Jason. "Hey, where do you think I could get a pair like that?"

Parker gritted his teeth. He was wearing sneakers from Payless. The worst thing that could happen to a kid was to get caught wearing sneakers from Payless.

"My uncle brought them back from England, so you probably can't get them. Sorry."

"He bring you that shirt, too?" asked Jason. "It looks like something you would get at Kmart."

Caught again. Parker hated going to school with rich kids.

"Ouch!" he said. "You got me. Well, see you later."

Parker turned to go. He would walk away. He would stay out of trouble.

Jason stepped in front of him. "Come on, Parker. What's your hurry? Let's hang out for a minute."

"You know, Jason, I would like to, really, but I think I had better be getting back. If Mr. Ardigo finds out I'm gone, I'll be in detention for the rest of my life."

"Yeah, well, it's just that Adam and I have a question for you." Jason stepped right up to Parker. "What's it like being poor?"

Parker bit his lip. He would stay cool. "You know what they say, Jason. Money can't buy you love."

"Yeah, but it can buy a lot of other things."

Parker couldn't help himself. "Obviously, not a decent haircut," he said. "It looks like you got yours in a helicopter in the middle of a tornado."

Adam guffawed, but the smirk on Jason's face disappeared. Parker knew he had made a tactical error. Rich kids can dish it out, but they can't take it.

"Kidding!" he said. "I'm just kidding around."

"Oh, we know," Jason said. "You're a funny guy."

"Great! So we're cool?"

Jason shook his head. While Adam stood watch, Jason shoved Parker against a wall.

"I hate funny guys," said Jason.

Parker stepped back, but there was nowhere to go. He was boxed in.

"Come on, guys," he said. "This is stupid. Let's just go find the class."

"Wow. Now you're saying I'm stupid? You just don't know when to shut up, do you?"

Jason raised his fist and laughed when Parker flinched.

"See that, Adam? He's just a talker. Parker's jealous. He knows that we have futures. We'll go to college, and then we'll get killer jobs and make lots of money, and he'll be watching from the sidelines. See, Parker here doesn't have a future. He's trash and he'll always be trash. He'll probably end up in jail."

Jason leaned right into Parker's face.

"Just like his father."

And that's when Parker snapped. The fingers on his right hand closed into a fist and he punched Jason in the face as hard as he could.

Jason fell to the ground, and for a moment, everything was calm. Jason clutched his nose, Adam stared in disbelief, and Parker stood, his hands still clenched, shocked at his own outburst.

Then Jason pulled his bloody hand away from his messed-up nose and broke the tension.

"Oh, Parker," he said. "You are so dead."

Parker looked at Jason. Then he looked at Adam. Then, for a split second, he looked at June, who was watching horrified from the gift shop. Then Parker made maybe his best decision of the day.

He decided to run.

PROPERTY OF PROFESSOR J. ELLISON
CAHILL UNIVERSITY
UNEARTHED OUTSIDE TAL SALHAB, SYRIA 7/12/63
DOCUMENT B31771—TRANSLATED 2/65—10/68

VESIROTH'S JOURNAL, CIRCA 1200 B.C.

The war came to us.

I had heard of the battles, of course, when I went into town to barter for goods, and I saw the soldiers when I sold my crops in the city. No one could tell me what the war was about, though rumors abounded. Some said it was a dispute about land. Others thought it was a battle to control the river that sustains us all. Perhaps it was not about anything so practical. Perhaps someone's great-great-grandfather had insulted someone else's great-great-grandfather hundreds of years ago and everyone was still upset. Such things are what make wars.

I was a farmer, not important enough to be kept informed, too busy to find out for myself. The fighting meant nothing to me. It did not affect the seasons or the way the sun hit the soil or the way the sands shifted in the north. I was concerned only with my crops and with my wife and with my daughters. I had no time for politics. There was always work to do.

The day that changed my life forever progressed like any other. I was in the fields, the hot sun on my back. My youngest sat near me in the dirt. She was playing with a toy stallion I had carved from a spare piece of wood. I remember how she looked up at me and how she smiled. She was beautiful and young and perfect, and I adored her. When I winked at her, she giggled.

I cherished those moments, and I knew that when the workday was over and our simple meal was eaten, my family and I would gather by the fire. My hands would be sore and my back would ache, but my daughters would make up stories to entertain me, and we would all laugh. We would sing songs and play silly games. I would send the children to bed, and my wife and I would share a quiet moment, knowing we were blessed. My life was hard, but I would not have traded places with the sultan. I was happy.

My daughter went back to her toy, and I returned to my work. That is when I saw the soldiers riding toward the house.

I was confused. I was no one. Their war had nothing to do with me.

My daughter abandoned her toy and hurried to

meet them, her black hair flowing behind her as
she ran. She loved horses, and she had hoped
that the men galloping to us in a storm of dust
were part of a circus. She thought the best of
people, always. Children do.

I knew better. They carried torches and
swords. These men were part of no circus. I
dropped my scythe and I ran.

I grabbed my daughter in my arms and I put her
inside our little house. I knew my wife would be
grinding meal by the fire. I knew my oldest child
would be tending the animals nearby.

I gathered them together and told them to stay
inside. I took my copper ax, the finest tool I
owned, and I went out to meet the soldiers.

Surely, they would listen to reason. Surely,
they would see that we were no threat, that we
were a humble family with no ties to power, no
stake in their fight.

The men stopped their horses in front of me. I
raised my hand in greeting.

I was rewarded with a club to the side of my
head.

I fell to the dirt.

I tried to get up, but my legs would not stay
beneath me. I saw these men dismount from their
horses and kick in the door to my house. I
stumbled toward them, but I could do nothing as
they raised their torches.

The soldiers laughed as they set fire to my

home, laughed when my daughters and my wife cried out from inside, laughed when I tried to stop them.

I was weak. They batted me away like a toy. I fell again, and one of the men grabbed me by the hair. He held my arms behind my back and forced my face down into the fire. I could hear my own skin as it sizzled like cooked meat.

Thankfully, I blacked out. I would not have to hear my family's cries as they died.

Hours later, as I faded in and out of consciousness, I felt myself being dragged from the smoldering ruins. It was an old man. I tried to tell him to leave me where I was. Everything I had was gone. I had no reason to keep on living.

Before the words could come, the blackness took me again. That is how I came to travel with Farrad, alive but with all meaning for my life stripped away.

2

PARKER RAN DOWN A SET OF STAIRS and straight into the observatory's crowded main exhibit floor. He pushed his way through a group of Cub Scouts looking at a video slide show of the stars, and by a family with six (six!) kids in matching T-shirts who were testing out a set of scales that showed you how much you would weigh on Mars.

He ran behind a statue of Einstein sitting on a bench, and then up another flight of stairs, using kids and guides as shields, but he couldn't shake Jason and Adam. They were right behind him.

"You're dead, Parker!"

I know, thought Parker. I know.

He poured it on and got ahead of the kids chasing him. The next level of the building was a long hallway full of exhibits stretching in both directions. Parker ducked out of sight behind a massive globe of the moon. He stayed perfectly still while Adam and Jason rounded the corner and ran the other way.

A little kid with a toy rocket stared at Parker, and Parker grinned back, relieved. He was in the clear.

When he stood up, though, his jacket caught on the metal stand that was holding the globe up. Parker's grin vanished as the globe came spinning down and landed with a thud at the rocket kid's feet. Then it started to slowly *roll*.

Someone yelled, "Hey!"

Great, thought Parker. A security guard. Where was he when I was being threatened by my buddies Jason and Adam?

The guard ran to Parker, clutching his belt with his left hand so his radio and flashlight didn't bang into his legs.

"Don't move! Stay right there!"

Good advice, thought Parker. But not great advice. He ran again.

"Hey!" said the guard. Parker looked over his shoulder and saw that the huge globe was gathering speed and scattering people left and right as it cut a swath through the museum. The Cub Scouts scrambled for cover, tangling up the guard, who watched helplessly as the globe smashed into Einstein's bench and knocked the statue over.

Mr. Ardigo's not going to be happy about that, thought Parker. He ducked under a brass railing and burst through some closed doors into the planetarium, where the show he was supposed to be watching was just getting started. A machine rose up in the middle of the room and projected lights and colors onto the domed ceiling to make you feel like you were looking at space.

The show's narrator explained how far away the stars were and talked about how the different constellations got their names, and pointed out the Milky Way and the Crab Nebula. The seats were laid back so you didn't have to crane your neck to look up.

Parker didn't have time to enjoy the show. He ran straight to the exit on the other side of the room, the security guard on his tail.

"Parker!" said Mr. Ardigo from one of the seats. "That had better not be you!"

"It's not!" Parker said as he got through the exit door, just steps ahead of the guard, who had renewed the hunt with a very red face and a burst of not-so-good-natured intensity.

Parker ducked behind a wall, and the guard ran right past, barking into his radio.

Parker put his hands on his knees, out of breath from all that running. An old man stared at him.

"The scope of the universe," Parker panted. "It takes my breath away."

Parker had escaped. He had no idea what to do next, but the important thing was that, for the moment at least, he was safe.

"Hey, buddy," said a voice behind him.

Parker turned. It was Jason and Adam.

"We've been looking all over for you."

Parker ran once more, this time heading for open space. He slammed the handle on some glass doors and found himself outside.

The exterior of the observatory was even more impressive than the inside. There were walkways on every floor, with coin-operated telescopes mounted to the railings so you could look at Los Angeles. Girls posed while their boyfriends took their pictures in front of the city.

It really was some view. From here, LA didn't look half bad.

Parker stopped. The sweaty security guard was coming the other way.

He was in it now. If he went left, Adam and Jason would get him. If he went right, he'd run straight into the security guard. He was toast.

Parker didn't know the place's layout, but he knew that the levels were all connected by stairways. Piece of cake. He would jump the wall, land on the stairs, and run down to the bottom level. Easy. Elegant, even. Parker put his hand on the railing and vaulted over.

Except the stairs were on the other side of the building, and Parker had just launched himself over the edge of a cliff. The only thing there was a hundred-foot drop and some very unfriendly looking rocks.

Holy crap, thought Parker. Jason was right. I really am dead.

I have been with Farrad for weeks now.

He is an enigma to me. He dresses in tattered robes and worn sandals. He has no friends and mentions no family. Even his age is a mystery to me.

We never stay in one place for more than a few days. He trades household objects out of his battered wagon, earning just enough silver to keep us in food and his old horse in oats. I do not know where he comes from or where he is heading. He seldom speaks, and when he does he says no more than a few words at a time.

He has taken great care to nurse me back to health. He fed me broth until I was strong enough to take solid food. He covered my damaged face with bandages. He gave me clothes and a place to lay my head. At night we sit by the fire in silence. Farrad stares into the flames and thinks his thoughts. He has asked me no questions about myself, although he must know what happened to me. If he takes any satisfaction at having saved my life, he does not show it. His kindness to me feels less like a good deed and more like atonement for past sins.

I can think of nothing but my family and how I failed them.

One day, while Farrad was away trading, the grief I felt over the death of my wife and daughters finally overwhelmed me. I felt I could not bear another night of loneliness, another night of black dreams that ended in me sweating through my bandages and screaming myself awake. I had nothing to live for, and my despair was so great that I sought to do myself harm.

I searched for something, anything I could use to take my own life. Perhaps Farrad had foreseen my joyless mood, for the wagon was devoid of weapons of any kind, and even the sham ointments foisted off on gullible peasants as a cure-all for anything from coughing fits to baldness were gone.

In my desperation, I tore the wagon apart. Just when my mood was at its bleakest, my hands felt a weak spot in the wood of Farrad's driver's bench. I pried it open and found hidden within an ancient book, so old that at first I dared not open it lest the pages crumble into dust. I found my courage, though, and I opened the volume to read.

What I found astounded me. The book is an

ancient compendium of arcane magick, written
by hand and bound in some kind of hardened
leather. It describes something called
the Nexus, which is a force of magick that
surrounds everyone and everything. With the
right spells, potions, amulets, and talismans,
the book claims that it is possible to tap into
the Nexus and amass great power.

The book is the first thing, the only thing,
to hold my interest since the destruction of my
family. I became obsessed. I read it through
that night and put it back in its hiding place
before Farrad returned. Now, whenever he is
gone, I go back to the pages. They pull at me,
call to me even. They quiet the screams of my
wife and daughters when they threaten to smother
me. The secrets of the universe are contained
within them.

I am especially beguiled by the book's
concluding page. There is written a fragment
of an incantation that promises ultimate power.
The spell is incomplete, but it intrigues me and
haunts my sleep.

Perhaps in the Nexus I may find the peace that
eludes me.

3

APPARENTLY, MERCURY AND THE REST
of the observatory gods were feeling...benevolent.

Mr. Ardigo, out looking for his favorite student and for once
in his life at the exact right place at the exact right time, grabbed
Parker's arm and stopped him from getting all the way over the
railing and splatting to a messy death on the rocks below.

He stopped Parker in midair and dragged him back over the
wall. Mr. Ardigo didn't let go until they were both lying in a
heap next to the wall.

"Thanks," said Parker, his eyes wide with amazement. "For a
minute there I was in serious trouble."

Oh, thought Mr. Ardigo, you have no idea what serious trouble is.

"Suspended. Well, that's just great, Parker. That's just about perfect."

Parker stared out the window of the ten-year-old Saturn sedan as his mother drove. The car was once tan, but most of the paint on the roof and the hood had blistered off in the California sun. The back door on the driver's side was red, replaced after an accident years ago, but never repainted. His mother had assumed she would scrape together the cash to do it someday, but someday never came.

"You talk back. Your grades are terrible, you lost all your friends, and now you're getting into fights. Awesome. You're future's looking brighter every day."

"I don't know why I'm the one that's in trouble!" he said. "Those guys were beating on this little kid and I told them to stop and they turned on me! I should be getting some kind of a reward!"

"Don't. Don't even . . . Just don't."

Parker shut his mouth. His mom was wearing her Denny's uniform, and she smelled like French toast and pancake syrup. That meant that the school called her at work, and *that* meant that she had to get someone to cover the rest of her shift, and *that* meant that her boss, Antonio, was not happy, and that was bad news for everyone involved.

"When I think about what a pain it was to move just so you could be in a better school district . . ." She trailed off. A lot of people told Parker that he looked like his mom. They both had dark brown hair and hazel eyes. Nobody ever told Parker he looked like his dad.

"You know you broke that kid's nose, right? We'll be lucky if his parents don't sue. His dad's a lawyer. Or a tax guy. Something like that. That's just what we need."

She stopped the car at a red light. Parker looked up at a palm tree. In the movies, they seemed so glamorous, but they were everywhere in LA. This one was outside a liquor store with a broken sign.

Parker's mother sighed. Her sarcastic tone was gone when she spoke again.

"I'm trying, Parker. I'm trying so hard, but I'm doing it all alone, and you're not helping me. It's just . . ." She looked out her window. "It's just not working."

The light turned and the car drove on, the two of them sitting in silence.

"I talked to your principal, and I talked to your school counselor, and they suggested that maybe it might be a good idea if you spent some time someplace where you could stay out of trouble. Someplace with a yard and some fresh air where you could take a break and maybe make a fresh start. We thought that maybe if you stayed with your cousin for a while in New Hampshire . . ."

Parker was stunned. He had expected the usual riot act, the yelling, the empty threats. He hadn't expected this.

"You're sending me *away*?"

"No! No!" said his mom. "Just for a little while."

Parker couldn't believe it.

"It's hard for you here. I'm working all these double shifts, and you're alone half the time. It's not good for you. And you need some positive male influence in your life."

Parker let that one sit there. He knew she was talking about his dad, and he knew that she was right. Parker's father was nobody's role model.

"Let's just try it. Let's both agree that it's an experiment and that we'll both try to look at it like it's a positive thing. It'll be an adventure."

Parker sulked. "Yeah, New Hampshire is known for adventure."

"It won't be for forever. Just until things improve a little bit."

"So this is a done deal, then? I don't even get a say in it at all? I thought this was a democracy."

"Don't be so dramatic, Parker. You're not going to a mental institution. You're going to New England."

"Same difference."

Parker's mom's voice turned cold again. "This is happening, buddy, so you might as well get used to the idea. I've already talked to your aunt Martha and uncle Kelsey. You're going this weekend."

"This weekend? I can't go this weekend! I have things to do here!"

"Really? Like what, exactly?"

Parker opened his mouth, but nothing came out. He didn't have anything planned. Not a single thing.

"Really, Parker, what have you got to lose? What's here that you'll even miss? Maybe you'll like it out there. You certainly don't seem to like it here."

She had a point.

"And it's not like I'm abandoning you. You're going now, and then I'm coming out in three weeks for Thanksgiving."

Parker shook his head. He knew his mother. That was never going to happen.

"I am!" she said. "We'll spend Thanksgiving together!"

"Sure, unless you have to pick up an extra shift or you can't afford the ticket."

"I'll work it out."

"Or you decide to go see dad instead."

Parker practically spit the words out. His mother opened her mouth to say something cutting right back to him, but she took a breath instead. She let herself calm down before she spoke.

"Sooner or later, you're going to have to forgive him," she said.

Parker stared ahead.

"I'm not excusing what he did. It was stupid and it was selfish, and he's paying the price for it. We're *all* paying the price for it. You know, it hurts his feelings that you won't go and see him."

"He's a crook."

Parker's mother glared at him.

"He's the man I married. And when this is all over we're going to be a family again, even if it kills me."

They drove in silence for a moment. The button for the passenger-side window was broken. There was a Chiquita Banana sticker Parker had stuck on the dashboard in sixth grade.

"New Hampshire will be good for you, honey. It'll be good for you to have people around that are going to be there for you. It'll be good for you to have people you can count on."

"You can't count on anybody," Parker said. "They'll always let you down."

His mother drove on. Parker knew that she was hurt, but at that moment, he didn't care.

Tonight, Farrad came back from trading earlier
than I expected him.

He found me reading the book by the light of
an oil lamp. I was so engrossed in its secrets
that I did not hear him until he was already
upon me. He jerked the book from my hands and
began to scream, furious at my transgression
and betrayal. I had never seen Farrad display
any emotion at all, and to see him so angry was
a surprise to me. At first, he railed against
me, but soon his rant took on a different cast.
He began to warn me against using magick. He
said that any attempts to connect with the Nexus
would only lead to my ruin.

I listened to his outburst with a chastised
heart. The book was his, and I had no right to
take it. He had saved my life, after all. I was
in his debt.

But emotions I had never before felt flooded
over me, and my guilt became bitter resentment.
Who was this pathetic peddler to tell me what to

do? Why should I follow his example, when he was so clearly a worm of a man? He had nothing. A wooden wagon rotting from the wheels up. A load of worthless trinkets. A bucket of meal. A horse close to death. If he were to simply skim the surface of what the book promised, he could be swimming in gold.

I knew then that Farrad was a fool. I remembered the pages of the book and I raised my hands. I summoned up but a paltry sliver of the Nexus's power and cast my first spell. A ball of green light appeared in my hands, and Farrad was blown out of the wagon. He landed heavily in the dirt.

The book was mine. I climbed down from the wagon and leaned over Farrad. For a brief moment, his eyes flashed with anger, and he raised his hands as if to cast a spell of his own. I backed away, suddenly afraid. I sensed a great power unleashed in Farrad, as if I had roused a sleeping beast into action.

Then, as suddenly as it appeared, the fury in Farrad was subdued. He seemed tired and resigned and older than I had ever imagined. I approached him warily, and I pried the book from his hands. He stared ahead, powerless to stop me.

I felt the sting of my own betrayal as I mounted his ancient horse and rode off into the

night, but the promise of the book urged me on.
I had a new reason to live. I would find the men
who had slaughtered my family, and I would use
the spells at my disposal to make them pay.

4

PARKER STEPPED INTO HIS NEW
bedroom and dropped his bag on the floor.

"This is Martha's crafts room," said his uncle Kelsey.

Parker could tell. There was a sewing machine shoved against
the wall, and the quilt on the twin bed was handmade. The wall-
paper had pictures of flowers and vines, and it was torn at the
corners where the walls met the ceiling.

"I asked her to clean it out, but I think she just shoved most
of her stuff into the closet. Not a lot of space here. Still, it should
be big enough for you. Good thing you travel light."

Uncle Kelsey put Parker's duffel bag on the bed.

It was a farmhouse, deep in rural New Hampshire. The land
had once been a working apple orchard. There were still some
trees, and a battered old barn with a cider press, and a tractor with

a seized piston. The Merritts' house needed paint and new windows. The pipes groaned when anyone ran the water. It was old, but it was solid and it was big. It was a world away from Parker's two-bedroom apartment in Los Angeles.

"Theo! Your cousin's here!"

Uncle Kelsey ran a hand through his thick hair. He was a big man with an outdoorsy look about him. He had a goatee and work boots. His stomach hung over his jeans. He looked like a guy who knew how to get broken things to work again.

He crossed his arms on his chest.

"I know this is a big change for you, Parker. It's a big change for us, too. But there's no reason this shouldn't work." He paused for a moment. "I know it's been tough on you, with what happened with your dad and everything. I want you to know that you can come to me or your aunt, either one of us, if you have any problems."

Sure, thought Parker. There was about as much chance of that happening as there was for Parker's shoes to spontaneously transform into singing frogs.

He put his hand on Parker's shoulder.

"We want you to think of this as your home."

Parker didn't react. Uncle Kelsey removed his hand. When he turned around, Parker's cousin Theo was in the doorway.

"Hey, Theo," Uncle Kelsey said. "Great. You can help your new housemate get settled in."

Uncle Kelsey walked out and down the stairs in search of his wife, leaving Theo and Parker.

"Hi, Theo," said Parker.

Theo wore an MP3 player strapped to his arm, and gym shorts

and a Robert Frost Junior High T-shirt soaked with sweat. He had braces and a crew cut. He took the buds out of his ears.

"This is crazy," Parker said. "I mean, one minute I'm whooping it up in LA, and the next thing you know I'm in the sticks. It's like living in the eighteen hundreds, am I right?"

Theo just stood there.

Parker took a breath and, for just a second, let his defenses down.

"I'm glad to see you, Theo. Really. You're, like, the only person I know in this entire state."

Theo shook his head. "The bus comes at seven fifteen," he said. "I get the first shower."

"Wow. Okay. You're going to show me around and everything, right? At school and stuff?"

Theo just put his earbuds back in and walked off.

"Theo?"

Theo was gone.

Parker looked at the nightstand by the bed. His aunt Martha had placed a framed photo there of Parker with his mom and dad. He remembered the day it was taken. They were on a trip to the Grand Canyon. His dad had bought Parker a cowboy hat and a badge that said US MARSHALL. They were all smiling. Happier times.

All at once, the fact that he was separated from both his parents finally sank in, and a single sob erupted from Parker's lips. He clamped his hand over his mouth and stood absolutely still. He closed his eyes. He took a deep breath.

When he had everything back under control, Parker opened his eyes, turned the picture facedown on the table, and started to unpack.

After weeks of searching, I found the soldiers
who destroyed my life.

They were in a tavern, drinking and laughing
and telling one another lies about great
battles they had won. They paid no attention to
me as I made my way to their table. Why would
they? I was just a peasant dressed in rags and
bandages. I was harmless.

Then one of the men jeered at me, and another
threw a piece of wet food at my head. I was
beneath them. I did not deserve to be in their
presence.

I closed my eyes. This was the moment I had
been waiting for.

I spread my arms to my sides, and I felt the
power surge through me. I had chosen a spell
carefully and had practiced it day and night
since I had abandoned Farrad. I would not trip
over the strange words. I would not hesitate. I
would not fail.

I took a deep breath and began. As I said the

words, my bandages fell away and the burns that disfigured half of my face were revealed.

Did the soldiers recognize me? Did they look on me and feel regret for what they had done to me and to my family?

The air turned cold, and smoke rose around me. The sounds of drinking and conversation gave way to panic as fear took hold. One of the soldiers, realizing too late that his fate was sealed, sprang at me with a knife. Before he reached me, my spell was done. As I finished the incantation, I closed my eyes tightly and brought my hands together in one mighty clap.

There was a roar, and then silence.

When I opened my eyes, I saw that everyone in the room was dead.

For a moment, my heart sank. I had tried to move beyond my anger, to let things lie. I had tried to think of my family and what they would have thought of my dark pursuits. I had tried to put their deaths behind me. But always the Nexus called to me. Always I had found myself turning the pages of the book, studying its arcane secrets.

And now, though my family was avenged, I saw that I had only brought more sorrow into the world. Did these men not have families? What of the innocents caught in my own war of vengeance? What would my daughters think of me now, surrounded by the corpses of my victims?

I saw then that these soldiers were but a symptom of a larger disease. The enemy was war itself, and I knew that I would not rest until I had ended the very idea of war.

My future is sealed. In order to forever end war, I must assume dominion over all men. I must rule the world.

5

REESE WATCHED THE NEW KID TWO tables over.

He was small and scrawny, even for a seventh-grade boy, but, man, was he confident. One day of school and he was already surrounded by admirers.

"Oh, sure, we had a box at Staples Center, so I got to know some of the Clippers a little bit. Blake Griffin, Chris Paul. One time I got to sit on the bench for a game. They play so much, though, and sometimes I just wanted to hit the bars on Sunset with my friends. A lot of them are in bands."

Reese knew that everything that came out of the new kid's mouth was a crock, but the kids at his table hung on his every word. Sheep, she thought. They'll believe anything.

"How did you get into *bars*?" Jenna Conroy asked, her mouth hanging open. That girl would believe anything.

Parker shrugged. "I know people."

Parker looked at Reese, but she immediately buried her head back into her art history book. She was an eighth grader, and she didn't want him to get the mistaken idea that she was interested in anything he had to say.

She turned the pages of her book slowly. She wished that Robert Frost Junior High actually taught art history, but no dice. The high school didn't, either. She wouldn't be able to take it until college. Until then, she would have to be content sitting through classes taught by teachers who didn't want to be there, and filled with dopes, airheads, soon-to-be burnouts, and class clowns.

Reese's mom had gotten her the art book, along with the poetry and the Russian novels. She had also enrolled Reese in a pile of classes outside of school. There were the viola lessons, of course, and the piano, and the French, and the extra math (Reese was already far, far ahead of her high school-age tutor, a kid with bad skin and rimless glasses, who spent more time texting his girlfriend than formulating quadratic equations), and the swimming (Robert Frost didn't have a pool, but they did have a new scoreboard for the football team), and the ballet (this one Reese actually sort of liked, although she would never, ever admit it to anyone), among others.

Reese's mom was hell-bent on getting Reese into a good college on the first try, and in her opinion, it was never too early to start pushing. Overachievement was not enough. Reese had to be stellar in everything, all the time.

After years and years of constant pressure, Reese was just now starting to push back. She still got the grades, sure, and she still went to the classes (sculpting! There was a sculpting class for a while there!), only now she did it with magenta streaks in her short black hair, and enough rings for any six emo kids. She wore sweaters with long, long sleeves, and she mumbled whenever her parents spoke to her.

All of this was designed to get a rise out of her mom. It failed utterly. If Reese's mom noticed any of it, she kept it to herself as she taxied Reese all over Cahill for extracurriculars. Reese was starting to wonder if she was going to have to actually start listening to goth or death metal, which would be a real sacrifice. In her heart of hearts, Reese remained a Taylor Swift fan.

"Did you ever meet any movie stars?" another one of Parker's new pals asked.

"Meet them? Are you kidding? When I was a kid, Selena Gomez was my babysitter."

Reese watched Parker's table out of the corner of her eye. Theo Merritt rolled his eyes and shook his head. Reese was pretty sure that somebody had said the two boys were cousins.

"Yeah, it's a shame I had to leave Hollywood, but I crossed some pretty intense guys, and the police thought it would be in my own best interest if I got out of town for a little while."

"Wait. Wait."

Jenna again. This girl was more gullible than a four-year-old whose uncle kept pulling quarters out of his ear.

"You're hiding out here? From a *gang*?"

"Gang is an overused term. Let's just call them a well-organized group of guys with similar taste in clothes. They thought I should join, but I had other ideas."

Reese saw the jocks before Parker did. They were eighth graders that had been her classmates since kindergarten. She wasn't sure why guys became tools when they got together in a group and put on uniforms, but in her experience, that seemed to be what happened. She would look it up. Somebody must have done a study on it.

"Wow," one of the eighth graders said. "Look at this, guys. We have a real action hero here."

Parker grimaced before he turned to face the jocks. There were guys like this at every school. Somebody had to run the places. Otherwise, kids might actually enjoy themselves.

"Me? Nah," Parker said. "I'm new here. I'm just, you know, trying to fit in."

The lead jock picked a Tater Tot off Parker's plate. Parker liked Tater Tots. Everybody likes Tater Tots. "Well, you're doing a bang-up job at it so far."

"We got off on the wrong foot. I'm Parker."

"Why, hello, Parker. My name's Evan..."

Of course it is, thought Parker. Of course your name is Evan.

"...and I'll be teaching you a lesson in how to respect your elders."

The jocks with Evan grinned. Reese saw Parker look to his cousin for help.

"You guys don't scare Parker," Theo said with a grin. "He's from the city. He's faced down guys with guns. To him, you're just a bunch of pansies. That's what he was saying before you got here, at least."

Parker turned red and started to stammer.

Cold, Reese thought, as the jocks escorted Parker up from his seat and quietly out of the cafeteria. Reese ate her lunch alone, and she finished the chapter in her book alone, and she checked the time on her phone. She still had five minutes before the bell. She picked up her book bag (black, of course, and covered with pins that infuriatingly did not annoy her mother) and walked out the back door to the alley behind the school.

She stopped at the Dumpster. Reese put both book-bag straps on her shoulders and pushed the lid open. There was Parker, covered in the remnants of today's lunch. And yesterday's lunch. And the day before's lunch.

"Thank you," said Parker.

"No problem. You know, you really should stay away from those guys."

"Yeah, thanks. I'll keep that in mind."

Parker slipped on some pretty rancid old tomato sauce on the bottom of the Dumpster but righted himself before he fell over.

"I'm Reese."

"Parker."

He held out his hand, but Reese just eyed him warily.

"Do I smell that bad?" he asked.

"No. I'm just not sure if I should be friends with you or not."

"Why not?"

"You don't seem like you're going to survive the week."

Reese hoisted her bag and walked away. She hated to admit it, but her mother was right about one thing: boys were nothing but trouble.

The tastiest books are always the hardest to come by.

The really good ones are banned, and all are rare. What sellers I can find are slippery men who live in the shadows and are not to be trusted. I could slash their throats, I suppose, but why bother? They would just be replaced. There is an endless supply of scum in the world, and I can't help but admire the survival instincts of the common rat.

I have rented a charmingly decrepit room in the city, and I toil alone until my eyes hurt from reading by the dim light of candles. I dress in rags, and when I go outside I cover my face with a filthy bandage so as not to show my scars. People avoid me. They assume I am a beggar, or worse.

They are right. I am worse.

My landlord pounds on my door and threatens to throw me out into the street. It might amuse me to summon a demon to drag him away, but there would be a mess, and the smell would linger for days. I take the prudent course and instead conjure a handful of silver coins. I pay him his rent and slam the door in his face. He walks away in a huff, with no idea how close to oblivion he has just come. There is a certain pleasure in living in ignorance.

In my centuries of study, I have learned many things. I have discovered magick that makes me powerful, and amulets that can be used as fierce weapons. I had practiced the arcane arts for only thirty years before I discovered the spell that would allow me to live forever. I am told that this knowledge is in the hands of only a select few sorcerers. I do not associate with my peers, although I know I walk among them. I feel no need to socialize with a group of magickal malcontents, all trying to outdo one another with tricks and amazements.

The key to immortality is mine, and yet I find it a trifling thing. War still rages around me. What good is eternal life if I cannot enforce my will on the world? Is a life never ending a gift or a curse?

I search always for the missing pieces that would complete the incantation at the back of Farrad's book. This is the ultimate weapon. This is the key that will make me the world's master.

The spell's creators are shrouded in mystery.

They are men discussed in hushed voices,
wizards whose past deeds are known now only
as myths and legends. According to the tales,
they were the Elders, the first sorcerers who
ever bridged the gap between our world and the
Nexus. They pooled their wisdom and between
them created the most powerful spell yet
in existence. Why did they never cast their
masterpiece? No one knows. There are theories
that the Elders were afraid of the power that
would be unleashed, and others that suggested
a traitor among them turned the Elders against
one another. Whatever the true history of the
Elders, their most powerful magick is to this
day unused.

Was Farrad one of the Elders? I fear I will
never know. I have searched for him, but even
with my resources I can find no trace. It is as
if the man has vanished from the face of the
earth.

No complete copy of the spell remains, but
bits and pieces float through the world of the
arcane and the occult. Through the years I have
collected all but one piece of the lost spell.
The last, missing fragment torments me. I know
it is out there somewhere. It waits silently for
me and me alone to find it.

I suppose there is no need to rush.

6

CAHILL UNIVERSITY WAS A SMALL
school set on top of a large hill. The grounds were well-tended
and the brick buildings were old. Classes were done for the day,
but a few students sat on the grass and the low, stone walls reading, talking, and enjoying the fall weather that they knew would
turn nasty in just a few weeks. A kid with dreadlocks played
an acoustic guitar under a tree. The guy in the CU sweatshirt
discussing politics with the pretty girl handing out flyers for an
upcoming rally assumed that his jokes about Congress distin-
guished him as the kind of witty, sophisticated, well-read college
man that babes found irresistible. In fact, the girl had little to no
interest in him. She was obsessed with a guy in her intro business class who got drunk at parties and then burped the entire
Pledge of Allegiance.

Uncle Kelsey parked the old truck in the university parking lot and got out along with Parker and Theo.

"I won't be long, guys," Uncle Kelsey said. "I just have to move some stuff in Hilliard Hall and stop by the administrative offices. They always have something for me to do over there. There's a snack bar where you can do your homework. They make pretty good chocolate-chip scones. Theo can show you."

He locked the truck.

"I'll meet you guys back here at seven. Try not to get in any trouble."

He winked at Parker, and Theo rolled his eyes.

Uncle Kelsey went left. Theo hoisted his book bag and went right.

"Do you want to wait for me, please?" said Parker, running to catch up with his cousin.

Both kids were glad to get out of the truck. It didn't have a backseat, so Parker and Theo and their book bags were crunched together with Uncle Kelsey in the front, and since Theo was barely talking to his cousin, the trip was awkward.

Parker caught Theo and they walked in silence. A Corvette drove by and Parker thought that he might as well try again.

He said, "Those are nice. A friend of mine in LA has one. We like to buzz up and down Hollywood Boulevard looking at girls. They have tons of power, but I like something a little more exotic, myself. I got to drive my buddy's Ferrari once...."

"Will you please shut up?"

Parker stopped walking. Theo continued for a few steps before stopping and turning to face him.

"I was doing all right, you know," Theo said. "Straight B's.

I made the baseball team. I'm not a starter, fine, but I'm on the team, and I'm *this* close to being able to hit the catcher from all the way out in left field, and people at school are actually starting to notice that I'm alive, but just when I finally, finally get something going for myself, you show up with all of your BS about Hollywood..."

"It's not BS!" said Parker.

"...and you ruin everything!"

Parker had never seen Theo so angry. He was turning red.

"Why couldn't you just stay in California?"

"I wanted to! You think I wanted to come live in Hick Town? I didn't have a choice!"

"Oh, that's right. A gang was out to get you."

Parker closed his mouth. He knew that the gang thing was far-fetched. What could he do? At the time, he was on a roll.

"You cause problems, Parker. Everywhere you go."

"That's ridiculous."

"Yeah? Do you remember the last time we were together?"

Parker did. Theo and his family had come to California to go to Disneyland when the kids were ten. They were all having a great time until Parker disappeared. Everyone was frantic looking for him, and his mom pulled in park security to join in the search. They eventually found him. He had sneaked into a cotton candy stand and had eaten so much of the stuff that he was rolling around in the bushes, clutching his stomach. They had to call it a day. Theo never even got to ride Space Mountain.

"Come on. That was years ago!" said Parker.

"And what about when we were nine and you pushed me off the roof?"

"I didn't push you! You jumped!"

"I jumped because you said if I didn't jump you would tell everyone I still wet the bed!"

"Okay, that was mean, and I never would have actually done that. Plus, it really wasn't that high."

"You always have to be in the spotlight. It always has to be The Parker Quarry Show."

"It's not my fault I'm charismatic!"

"Well, all I know is that my parents and I are happy living out here in the boondocks, and we don't need you screwing things up for us the way you screwed up your family."

That stung, worse than Parker ever would have thought. It brought up a lot of feelings that he simply didn't want to deal with. It hurt. Parker stared at his cousin for a moment. Then he turned and made a beeline for the nearest building.

"The snack bar is this way," Theo said.

As Parker walked, he took a key ring from his pocket and jingled it at Theo. "There must be something fun to do around here. It's a college."

Theo was stunned. "You stole my dad's keys?"

"I *borrowed* your dad's keys. I just want to do a little exploring."

"You can't do that! We're supposed to go get scones!"

Even Theo knew that was lame. He thought for a second and blurted out the nuclear bomb of threats.

"I'll tell my dad!"

Parker turned, ready to call his cousin's bluff. "Come on, Theo," he said with a grin. "No one likes a snitch."

Parker walked away. After a moment of indecision, Theo rushed to join him.

Against all logic and contrary to my better
judgment I have taken on an apprentice. Perhaps
I am growing feebleminded in my advanced age. I
am over three hundred years old, now. I think.

She calls herself Tarinn. She is a young girl,
an orphan. She considers herself a sorceress.
What she is is a pest.

She was sitting outside of my door. I assumed
she was begging for food or money. She was not.
She told me she was looking for the mighty
wizard that people in the city spoke of in
whispers. She wanted to learn. She offered
me her services as a cook and an assistant. I
pushed her aside gently, considering I could
easily have turned her into, say, a centipede,
and continued on my way.

She was there the next day. And the next. And
the next.

Last week I needed a fresh eagle's heart for a
particularly delightful potion. I was in a rush.
I had much to do. I always have much to do.

I stepped outside and Tarinn was, as always, there. Underfoot. In my way.

In my anger, I raised my hand to strike her, but when she gazed up at me, I paused. Everywhere I go, people turn their eyes from my ruined face. As if by instinct they seem to know I am a man best avoided. They fear and hate me. But this street urchin was not frightened! Her eyes were bright, and for a moment my mind was clouded by thoughts of my own daughters, dead now for centuries. I had assumed that I had banished all memories of my life as a farmer and a father, but now they came flooding back. After all this time, any feelings besides anger and ambition felt alien to me. Have I been so corrupted by the Nexus that I am no longer capable of feeling compassion?

I reached my hand down to her, and in an act of kindness of which I would not have believed myself capable, I pulled her from the gutter.

I made her an offer. Lodging and food, for her help with my experiments and study. She jumped at the chance and actually attempted to embrace me. I pushed her away, my mind clear once more. Tarinn is not my daughter. She is simply a tool in service to my goals. I will send her to do my chores, so I can more fully devote my mind to unlocking the treasures the Nexus still keeps at bay.

She thinks she will learn my secrets. She is mistaken. I will teach her worthless tricks and keep my true plans hidden. When she is no longer of use, I will destroy her or turn her back to the streets from which she came.

Maybe she will end up a centipede, after all.

7

PARKER PICKED A BUILDING AT
random and strolled in like he owned the place. Years of experience had taught him that was the key to getting into places he
didn't belong: act like you were supposed to be there.

Theo followed him. "Parker! Cut it out! We're going to get
in trouble!"

"We're not going to get in trouble."

It was an anthropology building, or maybe archeology. Parker
knew there was a difference between the two things, but he didn't
know what that difference was.

All he knew was that if he was looking for something interesting, and he was, he had come to the right place. The hallway
was lined with exhibits of old pottery and tools. Parker knew the
good stuff was around somewhere.

He stopped outside an office door and got out his keys.

As he worked, Theo started to sweat. "Stop it."

"I just want to take a peek inside."

"I'm serious, Parker. My dad could lose his job."

Parker found the right key. He slid it into the lock and put his hand on his cousin's shoulder.

"We won't get caught. It'll be okay, I swear. You're allowed to have a little fun. Theo, if you're this wound up at twelve, you'll be dead of a heart attack before you hit twenty. You have to learn how to enjoy life."

Theo thought this over. Finally, he nodded. He didn't really need his cousin's approval, but he didn't want Parker to think he was a wuss, either. The door opened and the kids stepped into the office.

"See, this," said Parker, "*this* is what I'm talking about."

Professor Ellison's office was a wonderland of fantastic stuff. The shelves lining the walls were overloaded with skulls, dusty weapons, and weird relics. The professor's desk was buried under teetering piles of unread mail and unopened boxes. No one had sat there for weeks.

Parker went right to the good stuff.

"Egypt, South America, Africa... There's stuff here from everywhere," he said, checking out a tiki idol almost as tall as he was.

Theo stayed by the door.

"Okay, Parker, you've had a look around. Can we please leave now, please?"

"Come on, buddy, hoist up your skirt and live a little. Where's your sense of adventure?"

Theo walked tentatively into the room. With the utmost respect for someone else's personal property, he looked over some ancient scrolls and a mad tangle of necklaces that seemed to be made out of gold and teeth. He shuddered at a dead monkey floating eerily in a jar of yellow formaldehyde.

"Creepy," he said.

Parker hefted a brass dagger and gasped when he saw a row of what could only be genuine shrunken heads. He got face-to-face with one. It was the size of a baseball. Its skin was jet-black, and its eyes and mouth were sewn shut.

"Too cool," he said. "Do you think anyone would notice if something went missing?"

"Yes!" Theo said, flicking the tag on a stuffed monkey. "It's all cataloged! Don't take anything!"

"I won't," Parker said.

Theo glared at him.

"I won't! I swear. Sheesh."

Parker put the dagger down and wandered over to a series of newspaper articles and Web site printouts taped to a wall. Some were torn and yellowed with age. Some were brand-new. He read the headlines aloud.

"'Disturbance in South Korea.' 'Strange Sighting in Istanbul.' 'Government Attributes Odd Reports in Tennessee to Methane Gas Leak.'"

Theo wasn't listening. He had found a door to another room and was checking to see if it was locked. It wasn't.

Parker squinted at an article featuring a grainy photo. It was a picture of a man holding some kind of a large metal cylinder. The photo had been crossed out with a red marker.

"'Tanzanian Miners Make Unusual Discovery.'"

Parker reached for the clipping. Just before his fingers touched it, he stopped. There were voices coming from outside the office door.

Tarinn has been with me for fifteen years now.
The time slips away like rain sloshing down a
gutter.

She has grown to be a capable and determined
woman, and she has surprised me by earning
my grudging respect. She is not my equal,
naturally, but she studies for long hours and
she has learned much. Perhaps someday she will
be something more than worthless.

For the first time in hundreds of years, I
have a source of true companionship. Against
my will, I find myself somehow drawn into
discussions with her of the nature of the
Nexus, and we argue over our differing views
of the power the Nexus affords. Tarinn grows
increasingly convinced that overexposure to
the Nexus erodes the soul, and that magick used
in anger will lead to one's own destruction.
What does she know about anger? She is naïve.
Perhaps when she has lived as long as I have,
her thinking will be more clear.

Always I search for the conclusion to Farrad's spell. Always it eludes me. This failure is beginning to affect my usually pleasant disposition.

8

PARKER AND THEO BOTH FROZE.
Then, with the reflexes of twelve-year-old boys caught someplace they shouldn't be, they both scrambled into the office's
back room.

The room was for storage, and it was a mess of boxes and racks.
They didn't have time to close the door, so Parker and Theo flat-
tened themselves against the wall. A black dread grew in the pit
of Parker's stomach. Less then a week in New Hampshire and he
was already in deep, deep trouble.

The door to the office opened, and Parker and Theo could
hear a woman escort a man in.

"Where did you say you found it?" the woman asked.

"One of the guys on my crew dug it up," said the man.

Parker and Theo heard the thump of something heavy being placed on the desk.

"At first we thought it might be an unexploded bomb from over at the shipyard, but one of my guys was in the army and he said that wasn't it. Myself, I think it's probably an Indian thing, right? Some kind of sacred idol or something? I don't know. Anyway, I asked around, and people told me this kind of thing is right up Ellison's alley."

Parker scrunched up his face. His curiosity was killing him. Theo frantically shook his head no, but Parker couldn't resist peeking out the door. He had to see the thing they were talking about.

He couldn't see the woman, but he saw the man's back. He was wearing filthy jeans and a paint-splattered shirt, and he was unwrapping a dirty towel from the thing on the desk. When the man shifted, Parker could see that it was some kind of a container, a metal cylinder about two feet long, covered with weird engravings half-buried under the patina that came from being buried underground for a long, long time. The ends of the object were capped.

Parker couldn't tell if it was just his imagination, but the thing seemed to be faintly glowing.

"It's an interesting piece, that's for sure," the woman said.

"I was wondering . . . I mean, you think maybe it's made out of gold or something? Do you think it's worth any money?" asked the man.

"It's not gold," the woman concluded. "Gold wouldn't tarnish like this. I couldn't tell you if it's worth anything."

The man turned around, and Parker ducked his head back just in time.

"The thing is..." the man said. "The thing is, that thing's weird. I mean, it acts strange. We had a devil of a time prying it out of the ground. The pick Tommy was using flew out of his hands when he hit at it, and none of us could really get a grip on the thing. It's like it's made out of magnets or something. I put it in the back of my truck, and my dog just sat there growling at it. It's just...weird."

"Well, like I said, the professor's away at a dig until Wednesday. If you like, you could just leave it here."

"That's fine by me. I'll be happy to get rid of it, to tell you the truth, even if it *is* worth a few bucks. Whatever that thing is, it gives me the creeps."

The woman led the man out and shut the door, leaving Parker and Theo alone in the office. Home free.

But one of the straps on Theo's book bag was caught on something. He gave it a mighty tug and pulled an entire rack of iron spears over. They clanged when they hit the floor, making slightly less noise than a plane crash might.

Parker and Theo braced for the worst, but they were okay. The assistant and the man had gone.

Parker smirked at Theo, who shrugged back. Parker went back to the other room as Theo started to pick up the spears.

Parker saw the metal canister on Professor Ellison's desk. He walked over and put his hand near the object before pulling it away. He couldn't stop staring at it.

In the back room, Theo struggled with the spears. He would

get them all upright, only to see one tip over into the next, causing all the spears to go down again. He was contemplating the idea of just leaving the stupid things on the floor when he noticed something strange about the wall behind the rack.

It was shimmering.

Not a whole lot, but walls don't usually do that at all, so even a little bit of shimmering is bizarre.

Theo reached out his hand, mesmerized. When his fingers touched the wall, Theo was blown backward as if he had touched an electric fence. He hit the floor on his back, the papers from his book bag flying around him.

Theo just stayed there for a moment, catching his breath. Then he got to his feet and crammed his homework back into his bag, never taking his eyes off that glistening wall.

He ran to the other room, where he found Parker zipping up his own book bag.

Theo grabbed his cousin's arm.

"We have to get out of here. Now."

"Right behind you," said Parker.

Parker turned off the office lights before he closed the door. The towel was still on Professor Ellison's desk.

The weird container it had once covered was gone.

The spell is mine!

In the commission of her daily chores, Tarinn stumbled upon a tattered book that had fallen into the hands of a novice wizard. The intellectual titan had attempted to cast the spell fragment but managed only to annihilate himself in a burst of fire.

Tarinn handed me the book, triumphant. She knows that I search for something, but in our years together I have managed to keep my true aims hidden. She thinks bringing me this book will endear her to me. In fact, it only underscores the fact that I no longer need her.

I hold the book in my hands and I run my fingers over its charred pages. I can feel the strength that courses within. Soon, the world will be mine.

B66015

I should have known that I could not keep
my plans from Tarinn forever. I admit now I
underestimated her hunger for knowledge. She
grows more powerful every day, and I begin to
suspect that someday her connection to the Nexus
will rival my own.

   She watched me for days as I pieced together
the spell fragments, experimenting with
different orders. Finally, she made her own
calculations and realized what the spell was.

   She was horrified. She tried to reason with
me. Me, the great Vesiroth! She attempted to
convince me that I am making a mistake and will
grow to regret the path I have chosen, as if I
had not spent centuries formulating my plans
for a world at peace, with me as its sovereign.
Tarinn could never understand the wisdom of my
true goal. She once viewed the Nexus as an aid
to mankind, but now sees it as a threat. She is
convinced that no one can control magick this
strong.

   She is a fool. I have put all weakness
behind me.

   When she saw I had no intention of backing
away from a lifetime of work, she snatched the
pages from my table and ran to the fire. All
reason fled from me. Furious, I cast a spell

of binding that swept Tarinn up and violently pinned her high against a wall. My rage knew no bounds. The papers fell to the floor as I raised my hands again, intent on reducing my apprentice to ash. As the temperature in the room rose, Tarinn's eyes grew wide with horror.

In all the time Tarinn was with me, she had never shown fear in my presence. Tarinn alone seemed to see past the thing I have become and glimpse the man I once was. Now, she was like all the rest, cowering in the company of a thing driven past reason by dark magick.

What had I become? Was I truly now a monster, bringing nothing but sorrow to anyone who would dare approach me? I lowered my hands, and Tarinn fell to the stone floor with a thud. I gathered my papers while she crawled to the door. When I turned back, she was gone, and with her the last vestiges of anything within me that could be considered human.

I have no further need of her. I can run my own errands and cook my own food. Let her go back to her children's tricks and illusions. Simpletons like her should leave the real magick to men of vision.

I am Vesiroth. I stand alone.

9

PARKER DRANK A COKE AND PONDERED
his next move.

He had been futzing with his stolen container for hours in his
room, with his door shut and his blinds closed, in what might be
considered to be a waste of a perfectly good Saturday. He looked
at the mess he had made so far. A hammer, a rusty saw, and a
monkey wrench were laid out next to him on the bed. He had
tried banging on the canister, and sawing at it, and prying at the
caps. Nothing worked. As far as he could tell, he hadn't even put
a scratch on the thing. It just would. Not. Open.

He put the can of soda back on the table and hoisted the metal
cylinder. Heavy, he thought. Well made. The endcaps turned, but
no matter how much he tried, they didn't unscrew. The etched
markings on the canister's sides were deeply grooved, and if you

squinted at them, they glowed slightly green. What could make it do that? Emeralds, maybe? Whatever was inside there was something special, he just knew it.

He wiped his hands on his jeans and picked up a flat-head screwdriver. After a moment's consideration, he jammed the screwdriver's tip into the slight gap where one of the thing's end-caps met its body. He pried at it with all his might, but nothing happened. Well, if there was one thing that Parker had learned in almost a full half a year of junior high school, it was that sometimes what was called for was sheer brute force. He set the canister on the floor, inserted the screwdriver, and stepped on it, applying every ounce of his one hundred and eleven pounds. Parker thought that the cap actually gave a little, so he stepped down harder. Suddenly, an arc of blue electricity came off the thing. The lightning made a sound like a bug zapper as it traced the walls, floor, and ceiling of the room. When it touched the overhead light, the bulb inside exploded, plunging the room into darkness.

Parker took the screwdriver out and the lightning subsided. He was, frankly, more than a little freaked out. He could smell the burning ozone in the air.

He reached out to touch the canister again and there was a knock on his door.

"Parker? You in there?"

Theo. Why not? thought Parker. The guy did live here.

"Hang on! I'm . . ."

"You're what?"

Parker couldn't think of anything he might be doing that wouldn't make Theo suspicious, so he gathered up the canister and the tools, wrapped them in his blanket, and threw them on the bed. "Nothing. Come on in."

Theo opened the door to find Parker standing by the bed.

"What are you doing in here in the dark?"

"Just, you know. Thinking."

"Thinking? Thinking about what?"

"Just thinking."

Theo jammed his hands into his pockets and stepped carefully into the room. He spent a few moments looking around. There wasn't much to see.

"I got the keys back to my dad. He didn't even know they were gone."

"That's good," said Parker.

"Yeah," said Theo. "Yeah."

He walked over to the bed. Parker cast a worried eye down to his blanket, but Theo didn't sit. He turned to Parker.

"Look," he said. "I'm sorry about what I said yesterday and just, you know, about how I've been treating you in general since you got here. I know that what happened in your family wasn't your fault. It must be tough to move three thousand miles away from all your friends and your mom and everything that you know."

Parker was more than a little surprised.

"It is," he said. He meant it.

Theo ran a hand through his own hair.

"So, anyway, me and a couple of guys I know are going over to this go-kart track in Tramerville, and, you know, if you want, you can come along. If you want."

"Yeah! Great! Absolutely!" said Parker. "Just let me get changed."

Theo stared at his cousin.

"You don't have to wear a tux. It's a go-kart track. In *Tramerville*."

"Well, yeah, but still. There might be girls there."

Theo rolled his eyes.

"Fine. Whatever. I'll wait."

Before Parker could stop him, Theo threw himself down on the bed. He hit his elbow on something hard and grimaced. Theo's face fell.

"Parker," he said. "What's under here?"

I performed the ritual alone, near my new
lodgings deep in the empty desert. No one was
there to witness the greatest act of the world's
most powerful sorcerer. I need no audience. I
crave no glory.

I dug the pit and lined it with rare jade
as the book demands. I set the burning sulfur
in bowls of obsidian facing the north, south,
east, and west. I garbed myself in robes covered
in runes that were ancient even before this
continent had a name.

I fasted for nine days and nine nights,
sitting motionless by the pit's edge. When my
mind wandered, I dug a golden spike into my leg
to regain focus.

At midnight on the ninth day, I stood. My body
was weak with hunger, but my will was girded
with iron. There was no turning back. My time
was at hand. I would succeed where every other
man who had ever lived had failed.

I chanted the age-old spell. My eyes filled

with smoke as the words took effect. The ground beneath me shifted, but I was not deterred. When the moon reached its highest point in the night sky, I said the last words and I plunged the sword into the pit.

The earth responded with a roar and I was thrown through the air. I heard the low, moaning sound of pain, and I staggered back to the pit.

Through the gloom of smoke and the stench of hellfire, I saw him in his first moments of forming. He was shaped as I am, and he had the features of my face. He was clothed in robes as black as the blackest reaches of the night sky.

He rose before me, floating above the ground in a cloud of mist. He was a creature of untold power. I admit that even I was awed by the sight of him, and even I was visited by doubt. Was he a thing that could not be controlled? Had I created a beast that would destroy me? Was Tarinn right all along?

Then my creation bowed his head and in his first words called me "Master," and I knew that I would have my way. I named the genie Fon-Rahm.

The world is mine.

B66015

His power is immense.

He has the gift of flight, and he has dominion

over lightning and smoke. He can cause men
to overlook him as if he is not there. He can
conjure objects at will. Men are like insects to
him. He is a marvel of magick.

I have spent weeks inside with Fon-Rahm,
teaching him the ways of man. He learned
quickly, drinking information and knowledge
like a child drinks his mother's milk.

In many ways he is a child. My only child.

I find myself weakened after creating
Fon-Rahm. I assumed it was temporary, but my
condition persists. I will study my texts until
I find the cause.

It is a small concern. Soon I will bring my
genie out to the city, and all will know the
glory of my creation.

I really cannot wait.

B66027
He will not obey!

I called him into being from nothingness.
Without me, he was just an idea, an
impossibility, a dream that could not be
real. I am his creator, the most powerful
man to ever walk beneath the sun.

And he will not obey!

When I felt that the time for books and
schooling was over, I took Fon-Rahm into the
city. He looked with wonder at the buildings

that towered overhead. The achievements of man were fascinating to him, proof that mankind is a race of artists.

I know better. I know that mankind is a race of killers.

I waited, and I watched him explore. I knew that soon we would come across some tempting target.

And soon we did.

The soldiers were blocking the street. In their arrogance they assumed that there were none more important than those in their own ranks. Everyone else in the city was there simply to be bullied and spit upon. These were men just like the men who killed my family.

My time had come.

I smiled at my creation. Fon-Rahm had been called forth from the void to be my sword. With his might I would be ruler of all men. War would be a thing of the past.

I issued my command. Fon-Rahm was to wipe the soldiers from the face of the earth.

And he would not obey.

I spoke again, with more force. He was to kill these men, with no mercy. Their deaths would be an example to all armies of my awesome might. To defy me would bring about their destruction.

He would not obey.

Fon-Rahm spoke. He told me that he would not

kill a human being, any human being. He would not submit mankind to my rule. He said that man must be free to make his own decisions, for good or ill. A world ruled by a wizard was a prison.

I was enraged. I spit at him to do what I commanded. I was his master! He was nothing, a clump of sand in a hole I dug in the desert. He would bend to my will!

But he would not obey.

I heard laughter. The soldiers had heard my pleas, and they saw me, an old man with half a face, begging an empty space in the air to do his bidding.

Humiliated, I returned to my books with greater intensity than ever before. What had gone wrong? Why was my creation weak?

I found my answer. The spell demanded that I create Fon-Rahm using a shard of my own life force. A portion of the power that gives me life and energy was taken from me and went into the genie. It gave him life, and it gave him power that was no longer mine. That life force was charged with my thoughts and emotions at the exact moment it was transferred to my creation. In my excitement and naïveté, I had called on the most pure and incorruptible parts of myself, the memories of my wife and children, parts years dormant but not yet extinguished. I know now that Fon-Rahm represents me at my most merciful. Goodness and mercy were built into him, and they would always come before any commands to subjugate man.

I had failed. On every level, my creation was inadequate.

A rare misstep. I wash my hands of this pathetic creature. If this genie will not obey me, I will create another who will.

10

AS PARKER FAILED TO FIND AN explanation about the stolen container that would satisfy his cousin, a black Cadillac Escalade stopped at an intersection outside of Cahill. Another car pulled up behind it. The light changed, but the Escalade didn't move. The car behind honked, waited, and then pulled around the big Caddy and drove off.

The driver of the Escalade rolled down his window. He was a tall man with blond hair and deep, cold blue eyes. His jaw was clenched. He stared intensely out at the landscape as two passengers in the truck's backseat argued. Like him, they wore black suits with no ties. One was from Spain and the other from Thailand, but they spoke in a shared language any linguist would tell you had been dead for generations.

As their argument grew more heated, the driver raised his hand. His passengers instantly shut up.

The driver reached down and pulled a coat aside to uncover a tablet on the passenger seat. It was about the size of a laptop computer, and it seemed to be made of the same metal and to be from the same era as Parker's canister.

The driver closed his eyes and placed his hand over the tablet. Slowly, the metal plates on its surface began to rearrange themselves. When they stopped moving, the plates had formed an arrow that pointed to the right.

The driver covered the tablet and rolled up his window. The Escalade drove through the red light and made a right turn.

I returned to my pit and I chanted again.

I had learned my lesson well. This time I summoned the darkest and most cruel parts of my nature. I would not repeat the mistake I made with Fon-Rahm. This creature was to be cold-blooded and without mercy. He would follow my instructions completely, without pity for the deluded humans I was born to rule. He would respect the power of fear.

My new creation was born in a ball of fire, and as he rose to meet me, flames engulfed him. His robes were red. I was surprised to find that he, like Fon-Rahm, resembled me, but where Fon-Rahm adopted a look of deep contemplation, my new son wore a sneer.

He was perfect.

I called him Xaru. He and I will reign over this world. Men will cower in fear before us.

B66051

Xaru has proven to be every bit the student that Fon-Rahm was.

I am fascinated in the differences between my two creations. Fon-Rahm is always willing to give man the benefit of the doubt. He takes for granted the fact that man is, at his heart, good. Xaru scoffs at the idea. To him, man is an animal to be tamed.

Unlike his older brother, Xaru is not content to sit inside. While Fon-Rahm pouts in his corner, watching us like a chaperone, Xaru paces. He is restless. Energy radiates off him, and he seems eager to follow my every command.

He, like Fon-Rahm, calls me Master, but in Xaru I sense defiance and anger. I see him often watching the fire, delighting in the way it consumes everything it touches. I have told him to wait, that soon his power would be unleashed, but I feel his patience is coming to an end.

Xaru craves violence. He is far more my son than Fon-Rahm.

We are going to have lots and lots of fun together.

11

THEO STORMED OUT OF THE HOUSE.
Parker followed him, the canister cradled in his arms like a baby.
A heavy, weird, metal baby.

"I had to take it! It was like it was calling to me! It was like I
was supposed to take it!" Parker said.

"You mean you were supposed to *steal* it?"

"Who said I stole it?"

"It's not yours, is it?"

"It was buried in the ground! It's not anybody's!"

"We have to take it back," Theo said. "Today."

"Just let me have a little time with it."

"Today."

"Let me get it open, at least. I won't keep it, I promise. This is
something special. It's important. I just have to find out. If I give

this thing up without ever knowing what's inside of it, I'll never think of anything else for the rest of my life."

Parker planted himself in front of his cousin.

"Let me keep it for the rest of the weekend," he said. "No one will even know it's gone until Monday. Come on. Please."

Theo shook his head. It was just like Parker, he thought, to put him in this position. Parker was the one causing all the trouble, and now he was making Theo feel guilty about doing the right thing.

Parker said, "We'll take it back on Monday before school. First thing."

Theo sighed. "First thing on Monday. You swear it?"

"Absolutely. You have my word."

Theo threw up his hands. "I guess that's okay," he said.

Parker smiled. He had always been able to talk his way out of stuff like this. It was a gift. Poor Theo never stood a chance.

Theo looked at the canister.

"Can I see it?"

Parker handed it over and Theo hefted it.

"There's a crowbar in the barn," he said. "Under the screw jars."

"Great!" said Parker. As he ran to the barn, Theo walked to the side of the house for his mountain bike. He cradled the canister in one arm and pushed off.

Parker saw his cousin stand on the pedals.

"Hey! Theo!"

Theo started down the long dirt driveway. Parker chased after him.

"You said I had until Monday!"

"Yeah," said Theo, building up speed. "I say a lot of things I don't mean."

Parker chased Theo down the driveway, past the mailbox, and onto the street. He got about fifty yards before Theo faded off into the distance, leaving Parker panting by the side of the road. The six-year-old girl who lived next door to the Merritts gawked at him from the seat of her pink-and-purple Disney bike. It had training wheels, laser streamers, and a white basket with pictures of princesses on the front.

Parker waved to her.

After months of silence, Tarinn came to me. She had heard of a demonic sorcerer that had gone mad in the desert, and wanted to assure herself it was not her old benefactor, Vesiroth. So nice to have company! I offered coffee and pastries, which she rudely refused, and with great pride I presented Tarinn with Xaru and his sulking elder brother, Fon-Rahm. I was sure that when she saw the majesty of my creations she would finally understand my work. Instead, she was horrified.

She felt her fears confirmed: I had gotten too close to the Nexus, and the exposure had driven me insane. She said she could see the change in me from just weeks before. This is, of course, ridiculous. Would a madman have accomplished such miracles? I have never felt more in control of my mind.

Tarinn was also different. Her brush with death had changed her. Her smile was gone, replaced with a look of grim purpose. She

shunned my genies and issued me a warning.
A warning! From a second-rate conjuror not fit
to change my sheets! She told me that if I did
not contain my genies, she would. As if she had
that kind of power! I am the great Vesiroth, who
cannot die. I was destined to crush this world
under the heel of my shoes.

I dismissed Tarinn, and she left me with one
glance behind her. Was it pity in her eyes, or
hatred? No matter. I need counsel from no peer.
With Xaru at my side I will be unstoppable.

When Tarinn was gone, I felt a weakness
well up inside of me. I collapsed to my knees,
and Xaru had to help me back to my room. The
transfer of power that had brought forth
Fon-Rahm and his brother has left me fragile
and in a pitifully debilitated state. The power
that is rightfully mine will remain in my
creations until they are destroyed, and they
will never be destroyed. They sap my potency
with their very existence.

No matter. There are only two. I have strength
enough to do what needs to be done.

12

THEO GRIPPED THE CANISTER UNDER
his arm. It was awkward to carry, but doable, and he might as
well get used to it. He was planning on going out for football
the next year.

He did a double take when he heard Parker behind him.

"Come on, Theo! Wait!"

He turned, incredulous, to see Parker on Suzie McLanahan's
bike, pedaling furiously.

Theo groaned. "Give it up, Parker. I've been running wind
sprints all fall. I'm a trained athlete."

"Yeah, trained to sit on the *bench*."

Theo turned off the pavement and onto a dirt bike trail, picking up his pace and leaving Parker and his tiny, tiny bike in the
dust.

Okay, that was a tactical mistake, thought Parker as he followed his cousin off road. Shouldn't have mentioned the bench.

As Parker pumped the bike's pedals, the black Escalade passed him going the other way, the two men in back still arguing in their dead language. The driver heard a scraping sound and uncovered the metal tablet in the seat next to him. The plates on the tablet's surface rearranged themselves again, this time pointing directly at Parker and Theo.

The driver slammed on the brakes. His unbelted passengers hit the backs of the front seats as he executed a perfect bootleg turn in the middle of the road. He turned onto the bike trail, lined the Caddy up with the kids, and stepped on the gas.

Parker was already winded. Too much TV and not enough physical exertion, he thought. He shouldn't have quit soccer. When he was nine.

As he huffed and puffed, Parker heard the black Cadillac pull up alongside him. Weird, Parker thought. The Escalade was bouncing over brush and rocks on a trail meant for bikes, not cars.

And it was getting awfully close.

The Escalade swerved slightly in at Parker, almost hitting him.

Parker slammed his fist into the side of the truck.

"Back off!" he screamed. "Share the road!"

The driver of the truck rolled down his window. He smiled apologetically at Parker, and then he stuck a machine gun out the window. As the driver aimed the gun directly at Parker's head, Parker began to wonder if there was anyone in the world who wasn't really, really mad at him.

I have created a monster.

As with Fon-Rahm, I took Xaru to the city. We soon came across a group of soldiers marching through the streets. I commanded Xaru to kill them. I held my breath, fearing that Xaru would be subject to the same weak-kneed pangs of conscience that afflict Fon-Rahm. I am pleased to note that my concerns were unfounded.

With one concentrated blast of fire, Xaru annihilated the soldiers where they stood. The very ground underneath their bodies was melted into glass from the heat.

As the ash that was once the soldiers floated into the desert sky, I turned my face toward my son, Xaru. He was smiling, content, and finally free to express his only purpose for being.

It was as I had hoped. Xaru has proven more than eager to kill. What I did not expect was that his zest for bloodshed would be more overwhelming than my own.

With no soldiers left to slaughter and my
curiosity settled, I was ready to go home. I
strode down the street, gratified to see the eyes
of merchants cowering in their stores, terrified
by the carnage following me.

But Xaru was not finished.

He turned his power on the witnesses. There
was nowhere for them to run, and they died in
shock. Then Xaru burned the buildings that
lined the street. Fascinated, I allowed him to
cut down the running peasants like the scum
they were.

But then I saw three figures cowering by a pile
of rubble. It was a mother, trying in vain to
protect her two young girls from the destruction
that rained down upon them. The woman turned
her face to me, and a cold chill ran down the
length of my spine when I recognized her. It was
my own wife, somehow back from the grave with
our daughters, and returned to me.

I shouted at Xaru to stop before my family was
once again ripped from me in a wave of flame. My
wife and daughters must be spared!

The look on Xaru's face was one of pure
resentment. He obeyed my command, but it was
clear he would as soon vaporize me for my
insolence.

I turned back to the carnage, my eyes
searching madly for my family, but they were

gone. I ran up and down the ruins of the street,
but I could find no trace that they were ever
there. Did I really see them, or was this a
cruel hallucination to mark my descent into
madness? Was Tarinn right after all? Was I mad?

Xaru cast his eyes away from me. I must
remember not to turn my back on Xaru. He is
ruthless, single-minded, and filled with the
lust for blood. He is just as I made him.

B67020

I can no longer restrain Xaru.

My will is weakened by his very existence,
and I fear he has learned that my hold on him is
uncertain. I made him too well.

He takes a perverse delight in killing,
and it is clear that the city will become a
slaughterhouse if he is not contained. My life's
work is to be undone! Men were born to bow to me,
not the genie Xaru!

If Xaru is destroyed, the life force I have
placed within him will return to me and I will
grow strong again. As much as I hated to lose
such an exquisite creature of destruction, I
felt it prudent to make the preparations that
would cast him back into nothingness. I cast
the spell, but it failed to strike even a minor
blow. I am too weak. Xaru knows he has the upper
hand, and he will soon come to the well-reasoned

conclusion that he does not need me at all.
Clever genie!

Tarinn was right. I have unleashed magick
beyond my control.

Fon-Rahm has vowed to do battle, but he and
Xaru are too evenly matched. Neither genie could
destroy the other.

I saw Xaru reading my ancient books. What
could he want with the knowledge within? I saw
the spell he wished to cast and I burst into
laughter. Xaru is indeed my son and heir. He had
been hard at work mastering the spell I used to
create him and his cursed brother, Fon-Rahm.

Xaru wishes to create genies of his own.

13

THE ESCALADE HIT A RUT AND bounced high on its twenty-two-inch chrome wheels.

The bike trail was rough going, but the Cadillac could take it with no problem. It had four-wheel drive and a beefed-up suspension, along with the V-8 engine, a huge navigation screen, and wood trim in burled walnut and olive ash. The men in suits had stolen a very nice car.

A car, however, even a car as dope as this car, could not be expected to glide smoothly over the rugged terrain next to this particular Cahill, New Hampshire, bike trail, and this car didn't. The bouncing threw off the driver's aim, and his shots thudded into the dirt harmlessly instead of blowing holes straight through Parker Quarry.

Nadir, the driver of the Slade, swore. Not out loud, of course.

He had taken a vow of silence when he had taken control of the Path, and he was not going to break it over some undersize American teenager in a Dodgers T-shirt. He swore to *himself*. He had expected the lamp to at least be stationary, buried still, or perhaps on the shelf of a museum too stupid to realize what they had, but now here he was chasing two children down a trail made for dirt bikes, not three-ton luxury trucks. This was getting annoying. Nadir was not a man who welcomed annoyances.

He shut out the yapping of the Path members in the backseat and swapped out a clip for his submachine gun. The gun had once belonged to a police officer in Illinois. The police there had executed a raid on Nadir and his men, thinking that they were part of a terrorist group. The police were right, sort of. Nadir was a terrorist, all right, but not like any terrorist the cops had ever seen. After the raid was over and all of the police officers were dead, Nadir took the gun. He liked guns and he hadn't been able to bring any of his favorites with him, airport security being so tight these days. He and his men had to dispatch the policemen with swords and knives, just like in the old days.

Parker rode faster than he ever had before in his life. He could hear the Caddy roaring ever closer when he caught up with his cousin.

Theo was stunned to see him. He figured he had left Parker in the dust when he turned off the main road.

Theo said, "What are you—"

He didn't get any further than that, because Parker rammed his bike into him, crashing both of them into the wide drainage ditch that ran next to the bike trail. They tumbled down the side of the ditch, smashing their shins and elbows on rocks and hard ground as they fell, tangled up in their bikes. When they landed, thought Theo, *if* they ever landed, he was going to kill Parker.

They landed, finally, knotted together in a cloud of dry dirt. The canister from Cahill University slid to a stop a few feet away.

Theo gasped. He was already furious at Parker, and that was before the jerk ran him off the road. He could hardly believe his cousin was that intent on keeping the stupid canister.

"You could have killed me!" Theo said. "You could have broken both my legs!" He wasn't in any actual pain, but that didn't mean he was okay. He was certainly scraped and definitely bruised.

And the worst part was, Parker wasn't even looking at him. He was staring at the top of the ditch, some six feet up.

When Theo asked, "What is wrong with you, Parker?" Parker had the gall to actually hold up his finger in a "please be quiet I'm on the phone" sort of way.

"They're coming back," he said.

Theo looked up, incredulous. "Who? What's going on?"

"I have no idea," said Parker.

On the bike trail, Nadir calmly stopped the truck. He and the other men got out. There was no hurry. The children were trapped, unarmed, and they had the lamp with them. There was no one else for miles. They could take their time to claim their prize.

The three men took their police-issue guns and walked over to the side of the trail. They peered down through the dust into the ditch.

Parker and Theo gawked backed at them.

Nadir smiled and raised his gun.

"I can't believe it," Theo said to Parker. "You weren't making it up. You really do have a gang after you."

Parker just gaped. Think of something, he thought. You're good at this. Talk your way out of whatever this was.

"Uh, look, guys," he said as the three men inched their way carefully down the side of the ditch. They clearly didn't want to mess up their suits. "I, um, think maybe you've made a mistake, here? I think maybe you're looking for somebody else and not us?"

He looked to Theo, who nodded.

"Just a misunderstanding of some kind, is what I'm saying. It could happen to anybody. But whoever the guys are you're looking for, I can assure you, it's not us. We're in the *seventh grade*."

Parker really thought that last bit would sell them. Nobody would kill a seventh grader with a machine gun. That would be excessive.

The men, now at the bottom of the ditch, looked at one another. One of them turned to another and said something in a language that neither Parker nor Theo had ever heard. The other guy laughed. Parker smiled. Maybe he had gotten through to them. Maybe they realized they had cornered the wrong guys. Laughter is the universal language.

"Great! So . . . great! Then we can go?" he said with all the hope of a girl being asked to the prom.

The men stopped laughing. Nadir shook his head as he aimed his gun at Parker and Theo.

"Parker!" said Theo.

Parker and Theo scrambled backward, but there was no place to go. They were going to be killed and left there, literally dead at the bottom of a ditch.

Parker, desperate, grabbed the metal canister. It was the only thing within reach that could possibly pass as a weapon, and even then, it was still just a metal canister.

"Get behind me! This will block the bullets!"

"I don't think it will!" said Theo.

The kids shut their eyes as Parker held out the canister.

The lamp, Nadir thought. Finally. It would be his. He aimed at Parker's head.

Later, Parker would wonder why he twisted the canister, and, more important, how he managed to turn the caps on the thing in the exact right way, in the exact right sequence, and then he would come to the conclusion that the thing (or really, what was *inside* the thing) had wanted him to open it and had somehow given him the combination. That almost made sense, when he thought about it later.

There in the ditch, though, he wasn't thinking about anything other than how great it would be if he and his cousin weren't going to die. He was hoping, really, deeply hoping that someone, or something, would save them. You might even say he was *wishing* it.

Chaos reigns in the city as the war between my
genies rages on.

Xaru has created an army of his own, ten
brother genies that obey him and him alone. Each
of his genies is, as he is, a clone of me, but
the farther they get from the Nexus, the more
twisted they become. They are copies of copies,
with each flaw magnified. One genie, I know,
has four arms, and two are horrible twins,
conjoined at the head. One is made entirely of
swarming insects. I hear talk of the others,
but alas, due to my constrained circumstances,
I have not been myself witness to them. There is
a rumor, spoken in hushed voices, that there is
one more genie, a genie that Xaru creates as I
write this. The last of his brothers will be an
abomination, a monster so grotesque as to turn
all those who see him immediately into glass.
Impressive! If this is true, he will be the
greatest power to walk the Earth.

How proud I am of my son Xaru! If not for
my condition, I would be standing beside him,
laughing as my fellow men are cut down by
fire and magick. Xaru is right! There is no
reasoning with humanity! They must be put down,
one by one, until their wills are broken and
they beg for mercy.

Fon-Rahm, the fool, stands with the humans.
He is brave but deluded. He cannot win against
Xaru's beautiful genie army. I can hear them as
they battle in the skies above the city, and I
can feel the ground shake as they trade mighty
blows. Buildings fall. Fires burn. Humanity
is doomed, no matter how valiantly my first son
strives to fend off the inevitable. Men will be
slaves, perfectly docile pets for their genie
masters.

Some even know that this is for the best. In
the West, a cult has sprung up based only on
spoken stories of Xaru and his brothers, a group
of fanatic men who worship the genies as gods.
I applaud their enlightenment. They may be the
only wise men left.

The specter of my dead family haunts me. They
follow me everywhere now, always in the shadows,
never saying a word but simply staring at me
with pleading eyes. They are in my chambers
even now. I try to talk to them, begging them

to forgive me for not saving their lives, but my voice goes right through them, as if I were the one that did not really exist. The sight of them tortures me, but my time grows short, and I suppose I will not have to bear it for much longer.

Word has reached me here that Tarinn has struck a deal with the sultan. He knows that his claims to power fade like smoke from a dying fire, and he is desperate to keep his hold on the city. Tarinn believes that she can trap the genies in metal boxes. She has no chance for success. Her sorcery is strong, but she is no match for my magnificent creations. Let her try and be destroyed with the others for her impudence.

Would that I could be there to see her extermination at the hands of Xaru and his genie army. But I remain rooted here.

Each genie that Xaru creates further takes a piece of my own life force. I, Vesiroth, immortal wizard of untold knowledge and might, am reduced to a state of living death. I move as slowly as the oldest man. Each gesture takes hours instead of seconds. It has taken me days to write this, my final entry before I am frozen like a stone statue for eternity.

My only wish now is to see the triumph of horror over mankind, but it will have to go on

without me. When Xaru completes his last genie,
all my life force will be gone from me. I will
be frozen, a living statue, able to think but
not to act. Soon, I fear I will no longer be able
to mov

*[TRANSLATOR'S NOTE: The author's handwriting here trails
off in an indecipherable scrawl.]*

14

THERE WAS A CLAP OF THUNDER. BOTH
Parker and Theo agreed on this, later on. They didn't mistake it
for gunfire, either, because it didn't sound like gunfire. It sounded
like what it might sound like if a bolt of lightning had struck
about, say, two feet in front of them.

They didn't see what happened, because both of them had their
eyes squeezed shut in the completely unfounded belief that what
they couldn't see couldn't hurt them, but they could still hear,
and what they heard were gunshots. Lots of gunshots.

Parker, pleasantly surprised to find himself intact and unshot,
opened his eyes first. It didn't help. The ditch was filled with
a deep fog so thick that Parker couldn't see anything at all. He
walked a step and tripped over the now-open canister. It was

empty. He looked up to see Theo inches from his face. Theo looked as confused as Parker felt.

They heard the men yelling in their strange language, and then more gunfire lit up the fog. One of the men screamed, and Parker and Theo ducked as the man was thrown over their heads. There was a loud crash, and then another loud crash, and then Parker and Theo mashed their hands against their ears as the air was filled with the excruciating sound of tearing metal.

Then there was silence. Parker and Theo rose slowly, waving their hands in a vain attempt to clear away the fog. They stepped over the remains of their bikes and climbed carefully out of the drainage ditch.

The air reeked of electricity. The smell reminded Parker of an old electric train his dad had set up to run around the Christmas tree when he was a kid. His mom eventually made him take it down, because she was afraid it was going to start a fire. It was dangerous.

Through the rising mist, Parker could just make out the three men in suits as they ran away as fast as they could.

Parker stared, his mouth open. Theo tapped him on his shoulder, and Parker looked where Theo was pointing. One half of the black Escalade was in the middle of the trail, and the other half was lodged in the top of a maple tree. The Cadillac had been torn in two.

"Um, Parker?" Theo said.

"Yeah?"

"What just happened?"

"What just happened. Well, there's got to be some kind of a

rational explanation, right? I mean, maybe there was some kind of an electrical storm that . . ."

Parker trailed off. He could feel, behind him, some kind of a presence.

He looked at Theo, and Theo looked at him, and they both turned slowly to see what was behind them.

There, in the thinning fog, was a motionless figure dressed in billowing black robes. Smoke drifted out of his eyes, and lightning crackled down his outstretched arms and off his fingers.

Theo nudged Parker and pointed. The figure was standing, if *standing* is the right word, two feet off the ground.

"Uh," said Parker. He couldn't think of anything to add, so he repeated himself. "Uh."

After what Parker assumed was two or three weeks, the figure finally moved. Parker and Theo gasped as he landed gracefully in front of them. The figure crossed his arms and took a step toward Parker.

At least we won't be shot, Parker thought. We'll be fried by a weirdo with lightning coming out of his fingers. That's something.

But instead of vaporizing Parker, the genie Fon-Rahm knelt on one knee. He gritted his teeth and spoke his first words in three thousand years.

"You have freed me from my prison," he said in a voice gravelly from disuse. "I am bound to you. I am in your debt."

Theo gaped at Parker, and Parker said the first thing that came into his mind.

"Uh," he said.

"Oh, man," said Theo.

Theo pointed once again. Reese was in the middle of the bike trail, wearing a sky-blue helmet and sitting on an electric-assist bike her dad had gotten her for Christmas. This was the first time she had ever taken the trail, which promised to be a shortcut from her class at the community college (Latin! Useful!) to her house.

With all of that extra schooling, it was no surprise that Reese could find the word that Parker was groping for.

"Wow," she said.

15

PARKER, THEO, AND REESE SAT ON THE edge of Reese's bed and stared at the figure seated uncomfortably in the purple beanbag chair.

The room was predominantly pink. This was not something Reese could blame on her mother. Reese chose the color for the walls, and she chose the dresser, and the bookcase, and even the purple beanbag chair. In her defense, she was ten at the time. If she had a chance to remake the room, Reese would throw out the academic ribbons and trophies and paint the whole thing black. *That* would show her mom. Of course, it would be an awful place to sleep or read or talk on the phone. (Not that she talked on the phone much. Who would she talk to?) But all that would really be beside the point.

Reese supposed it didn't really matter. No one was ever in her room, anyway.

Until now.

"So you were trapped in that thing for how long?" she asked.

The genie shifted and pulled his robes away from his legs.

"Three thousand years. Give or take."

"And you don't want a sandwich or something?"

Parker looked at her like she had three heads.

"Really? We find an actual, swear-to-God genie, and all you can think to ask him is what he wants for lunch?"

"He's a fictional creature of Arabic folklore. What am I supposed to ask him?"

"Uh, where did he come from? Who were those guys that were trying to kill us? Why is he here?"

"These things would be beyond a child's comprehension," said Fon-Rahm.

"Who are you calling a child?" said Parker.

"This is so weird," said Theo.

They had debated what to do with the genie when they were still on the road. Theo wanted to call the police, but Parker wasn't super interested in explaining how he wound up with the canister in the first place. Besides, this was too good to turn over to somebody else. Even Theo had to see that. Reese suggested that they take him to her house. It was closest, and her parents were at work. They could hide out until they decided what to do. Parker readily agreed. Sooner or later, someone was bound to notice half a luxury SUV jammed into the upper branches of a tree and, quite frankly, he didn't want to be around to explain what happened.

The genie did not object when Parker told him the plan. Parker, Theo, and Reese got on their bikes and told Fon-Rahm to follow them, and he did. Parker looked back as they were riding and saw Fon-Rahm, his robes billowing in the breeze, as the genie glided over the trail. Parker had expected the genie to be looking straight ahead, but he was surprised to see that Fon-Rahm was actually staring directly at him. It made Parker uneasy.

They made it to the house with no problem. Now they were inside, away from prying eyes, and no one had the slightest idea what to say.

"You're a genie," said Reese.

"I am of the Jinn, yes."

"And we freed you."

Fon-Rahm raised a finger and pointed at Parker. "*He* freed me."

Parker perked up.

"Right!" he said. "I freed him! So he's mine!"

He turned to Fon-Rahm. "So how does this work? I get three wishes, right?"

Fon-Rahm sighed. He hated to say what he was about to say, but he had no choice.

"No," he said. "There is no such limit. I must do your bidding forever."

"I wish I could fly!" said Parker.

"I cannot make you fly."

"I wish I was bulletproof?"

Fon-Rahm closed his eyes.

"The scope of my power is boundless, but my ability to use it is not. Since you are my"—Fon-Rahm took a deep breath and practically spat the word out—"*master*, I cannot harm you, and I will not allow harm to come to you. I am compelled to obey you, but there are limits. I cannot change you physically. I cannot turn back time. If you see something you would possess, I can make it yours for a time. I can bestow knowledge in an instant, but it will fade in weeks or days. I cannot make another love you. I cannot change the human heart."

"Could you take out a few jocks for me?" asked Parker.

"Parker!" Reese said, appalled.

"I don't mean he necessarily has to *kill* them."

"I cannot harm an innocent on your whim."

"Can't or won't?"

"I will not harm an innocent on your whim. I will follow your commands, but I will not use my power for destruction and ruin."

Parker thought for a moment.

"Lame," he said.

"This is . . . This is . . ." Theo stammered for something to say. "It's unreal. Parker, do you realize what he's saying to you? You can have whatever you want. You can do whatever you want."

"That's true," said Parker. "I can."

There was a knock on the door. Parker, Reese, and Theo froze.

"Marisa? Are you home?"

Reese gasped.

"It's my mom."

"I thought you said she was at work!" said Parker.

"She came home! She does that after she's done working!"

Reese popped up and ran to block the door, but it was too late. Her mother pushed the door open.

Reese gasped. "Mom! I can explain!"

Reese's mother stood in the doorway and took in the scene. Reese knew she was done for. There were two strange boys on her bed and one exceedingly strange man sunk into a beanbag chair made to fit a ten-year-old girl. And, on top of everything else, Reese was supposed to be studying.

Grounded? No, not grounded. There wasn't a word for what was going to happen to Reese. Buried, maybe.

"Reese," said her mother, staring at Theo and Parker. "Who are these boys?"

Reese was surprised that her mother wasn't more upset.

"Uh . . ." she said.

"Um, I'm Parker? Parker Quarry? And this is my cousin Theo?"

"And why are you here?"

Theo raised his hand. Parker glared at him and he put it down.

"School project?" Theo said.

"Oh," said Reese's mom. "Oh. That's all right, I suppose."

She looked at her daughter, who was practically hyperventilating.

"It's fine, Marisa. You can have friends up here. I just want to know about it."

"Yeah. Okay."

Reese's mother looked back at Parker and Theo. "Do you want some carrots or iced tea?"

"No, thank you, Mrs. . . ." Parker started.

"Lorden," said Reese.

"Mrs. Lorden. Thanks, though."

"All right. If you want anything, let me know." She turned to her daughter. "Don't forget. Viola lesson at six o'clock. Keep the door open, please."

And just like that, she was gone. She hadn't seen Fon-Rahm at all.

Reese quietly closed the door behind her.

Theo pointed to Fon-Rahm.

"You're invisible!" he said.

"I'm not invisible. If needed, I can . . . encourage people to overlook me for short periods of time. It saps my strength, but it can be done."

"So . . . you're invisible," said Theo.

"No," said Parker, fascinated. "People just can't see him."

He flopped backward on the bed, knocking a pink pillow onto the floor.

"Okay," he said. "Okay. So, first, I think we can all agree that this is something we need to keep to ourselves, right? I mean, this is *major*. This is the biggest thing since . . . This is the biggest thing that has ever happened to anybody, probably. We can do whatever we want! We can be rich! We can rule the school!"

"I don't want to rule the school," said Reese.

"We can be rich!" said Parker.

"Stop," said Fon-Rahm.

The kids looked at him. Even squashed into a beanbag chair, Fon-Rahm was a commanding figure. His eyes gave off a faint blue light. He was stern and he was scary.

"I am Fon-Rahm, the first of the Jinn. When I was created, the mountains quaked and the skies turned black. I possess the might of ages. My power is a nation without borders. My eyes bring fear, and my hands, bolts of lightning. I could be the savior of the world or I could be its destroyer. I am not a plaything and I am not to be taken lightly. I will not be used for fun and trifling novelties."

Theo and Reese were suitably cowed.

Parker, however, sat up. He nodded thoughtfully at the genie and then broke into a grin.

"So," he said. "Have you ever heard of a Porsche 911?"

16

PARKER SKIDDED THE RED PORSCHE to a halt. Theo was thrown once more across the tiny backseat and into the window.

"Ouch," said Theo.

Fon-Rahm sat stoically in the passenger seat, staring straight ahead. His new suit fit him perfectly, unwrinkled even after Parker's insanity behind the wheel.

"You can relax now, guys," Parker said. "We're home."

Well, not exactly home. They were in some bushes in the middle of a field almost a mile behind the Merritts' house. Reese was already gone, dropped off near enough to her house so that she could get home on foot, but far enough so that no one she knew would see her get out of a hundred-and-fifty-thousand-dollar sports car being driven by a seventh grader.

She wasn't happy about it. It was going to be a long walk.

Parker and Fon-Rahm climbed out of the car, and Theo clawed his way out of the back. Theo was thrilled to be stationary. Until very, very recently, Theo never got carsick. Now he could barely look at the Porsche without getting dizzy. One more thing to thank his cousin for.

"Look at that!" Parker pointed at the 911. "Not a scratch on it!"

That wasn't even remotely true. The car was a mess. It was dirty and scratched, and one headlight had exploded when they landed their big jump over the cop prowlers. The jump had also seriously damaged the suspension, so the Porsche sat a little lower than it was supposed to. These little modifications made the car look like it was exhausted. If it were human, it might have sighed.

It didn't really matter. The Porsche was already disappearing, fading out of their existence and back to the Nexus. They could already see through the bumpers. In a few hours the whole car would be gone, leaving nothing behind besides tire tracks, confused policemen, and the smell of burned rubber.

"It's a shame we can't keep it," Parker said.

"No, it's not," said Theo. "You drive like a lunatic."

"I drive like a NASCAR driver." Parker turned to Fon-Rahm. "How long is that going to last, anyway? My new abilities, I mean."

"Days. Perhaps a week," said Fon-Rahm.

"When it fades away, I suppose there's nothing to stop me from wishing for it again."

Fon-Rahm gritted his teeth. "I suppose not."

"And I can always get another car. A Lambo next time, I think.

Or that Mercedes with the gull-wing doors. Of course, there's no backseat in either of those things. . . ."

"Good," said Theo.

Parker grinned. He had woken up with, let's face it, not a whole lot going for him. Now, here it was, less than ten hours later, and everything had changed. Everything he ever wanted was his for the asking or, more accurately, the wishing. From now on, things were going to go his way. He was exhilarated.

He was also wiped out.

"Let's go home," he said.

"Yeah, about that." Theo gestured to Fon-Rahm. "What are we supposed to do with him?"

"Way ahead of you, buddy. I got it all figured out."

Moments later, Parker, Theo, and Fon-Rahm were standing in the Merritts' old barn. At one time it had housed an imposing wooden cider press, and the sweet smell of apples still hung in the air. Now the barn was a catchall toolshed for Theo's dad. It was filled with long-handled rakes and pitchforks. There was a stocked workbench holding just about any kind of a tool you could possibly need, along with a half-finished remote-control plane that Theo's dad had tried and failed to get his son interested in. There was also a forty-year-old tractor that ran most of the time and a box of Christmas decorations that hadn't been touched in a decade.

Parker showed Fon-Rahm to an empty space in the corner.

"I guess you can sleep over here."

The genie stared through him. "I need no sleep," he said.

"Okay," said Parker. "Well, if you get hungry, I could leave you some . . ."

"I need no food."

"Water? Oxygen?"

"I am not alive in the way that you are alive. I am a creature of magic. You are merely flesh and bone."

"Yeah, well, I'm the boss of you."

"I'm going in," said Theo, looking warily at Fon-Rahm. "Are you sure he's going to be all right out here?"

"He'll be fine," said Parker. "He's a creature of magic."

Theo closed the barn door on his way out.

Parker yawned. "Okay, Fon-Rahm, get some rest. I have a lot planned for you and me."

"You try my patience, child. I am Fon-Rahm of the Jinn, not a toy."

"Whatever you say, Rommy old pal."

Parker put his hand on the barn door, but he stopped himself from opening it. He paused for a moment before turning back to the genie.

"What was it like? When you were in the lamp?" he asked.

Fon-Rahm contemplated this.

"It was like a dream," he said. "I could feel the centuries as they passed, but time itself was meaningless to me. It was, perhaps, like it was for you, before you were born."

The genie looked deep in thought.

"Now I find myself far from home, and in a world I do not fully understand. It is . . ." He searched for the word. "Difficult."

Parker knew the feeling. He was far from home himself, and often felt like he would never truly fit in.

He shook it off. He had an image to maintain.

"See you in the morning," he said. "Try not to destroy the world."

"You don't have much faith in me."

"That's true, but I wouldn't take it personally. I don't have much faith in anybody."

"Relying on others is not a sign of weakness. It is a sign of strength."

Parker shrugged.

"Huh. Well, great. I'll try to keep that in mind."

Fon-Rahm stood in his corner, his arms folded against his chest, as Parker walked outside and closed the barn door.

As he made his way to the house, Parker was struck with a sudden dull ache behind his eyes. He stopped and closed his eyes tight. The pain didn't go away. A headache, thought Parker; uncomfortable but nothing to worry about. If it got any worse he could always have Fon-Rahm conjure up some Advil.

He walked into the house through the kitchen door. Something was bubbling on the stove, and the whole house smelled like mashed potatoes. Parker pulled the lid off a pot to see what was inside, and he saw his aunt Martha sitting alone at the set table in the next room. She was Parker's mother's younger sister, but Parker thought she looked older. Her back was to him and she was talking on an old cordless phone.

"Why not?" she said. "When?"

She pulled absently at one of her apron strings.

"Well, get somebody else to do the double shift! He's expecting you to be here. I mean, it's Thanksgiving. . . ."

She turned her head to see Parker in the doorway.

"Oh! Parker!" She was suddenly all smiles. "Your mother's on the phone. Would you like to talk to her?"

Parker turned on his heels and walked away. He wasn't interested in hearing any more of his mother's excuses.

"Parker?"

Parker walked up the stairs to wait for dinner. His head was killing him.

17

THE ICE STRETCHED FOR MILES IN every direction, and a freezing wind cut through the barren plain. There were no trees or mountains or houses. The night held nothing but snow and the promise of a cold, cold death. It was forty degrees below zero.

The ice crunched under Nadir's boots as he stepped onto the tundra. He had been in the country for less than an hour. It had taken four flights to get to Greenland and, as he had slit the throats of the two Path members who were with him in New Hampshire, he had made the trip alone. The men proved worthless in the fight with Fon-Rahm. Worse, if they had survived they would have told their brothers in the Path about the fiasco, and Nadir could not let that happen. It would undermine his authority. It would show weakness.

He was angry with himself for losing Fon-Rahm. If he could have taken possession of the lamp, unopened, things would have gone much easier. Now the first of the Jinn was free and would have to be dealt with accordingly.

Nadir was not worried. Fon-Rahm was bound to a child. It would be no great challenge to defeat him.

Especially since the discovery here.

In the near distance, six men stood in a circle. They were bundled up in boots and thick gloves and coats with fur hoods. They carried picks and shovels, and one had a chain saw. As Nadir approached them, he could see their breath in the air and he could hear their teeth chatter.

The men stepped aside so Nadir could see what they had found.

It was a block of ice the size of a refrigerator, cut from the ground nearby. Inside, Nadir could make out some dark object.

Nadir pulled the guiding tablet from a bag on his shoulder. The metal plates on its face slowly worked themselves into a new pattern. The arrow pointed directly at the frozen object. Nadir put the tablet away and nodded. He stepped back as one of the men started the chain saw and cut into the block of ice.

When the lamp was free, two of the men placed it on a low stone altar set up on the ice. Nadir ran his hands over the metal cylinder. At last, his destiny was to be fulfilled.

Nadir raised his hand slowly and pointed to one of the men. The man nodded solemnly and stepped forward. He stripped off his winter clothes and donned a purple robe covered in ancient runes. Shivering, he knelt before the altar. He offered up a silent prayer and placed his trembling hands on the lamp. He twisted the ends first one way, and then another, until there was an audible pop and the hiss of escaping gas.

The man's face flooded with fear. The lamp opened with a roar and a storm of orange flame. Instantly, the sky was ablaze. The men turned away, their eyes burning. Some fell as the ground melted beneath their feet. Only Nadir kept his gaze fixed on the hurricane of fire in their midst.

The fire died down. Again the air was calm. When the smoke lifted, the genie Xaru hovered above the altar. His features were sharper than Fon-Rahm's, and where Fon-Rahm's robes were black, Xaru wore a brilliant crimson. He was like a more feral version of his older brother. At the sight of him, the men of the Path threw themselves to the ground in worship.

The man kneeling at the altar looked to the reborn genie, terrified. Xaru peered down at him, suppressing a sneer.

"You have freed me from my prison," he said. "You have my eternal gratitude."

The man simply whimpered.

Xaru looked to Nadir, power recognizing power.

"Of course, I am now bound by magic to do this man's bidding, and I am prevented from causing him any harm. While he lives, I am nothing but a slave."

Nadir nodded to one of his confederates, and the Path member presented him with a wooden box, lacquered black, its corners blunt from centuries of use, an image of a grinning skull carved into its lid. Nadir set the box on the ground, removed the rusting metal pin that held the lid closed, and reached inside.

He pulled out a small glass vial stopped with an age-old cork. The liquid inside was thick and oozy and as dark as tar.

As Xaru looked on, curious, Nadir removed the cork and let a single black droplet fall to the ice.

After a moment, the drop began to move.

The trembling man at the altar bowed his head. His whispered prayers grew louder as the black droplet creeped toward him. By the time it disappeared under his robe, his eyes were wide with terror. Soon, his legs were coated with the vile stuff. He swatted at himself, half mad with panic, as it engulfed his chest and arms, and his last scream was smothered when the black tar covered his face and his head.

Then, somehow, the goo began to contract. The kneeling man, now a writhing shadow, grew smaller and smaller. Finally, he was still, and all that was left was a single droplet staining the ice black.

Nadir put the opening of the vial on the ground, and with his finger drew an ancient symbol in the ice. At his command, the droplet rolled back into the glass tube. He replaced the cork and put the vial back into its box.

Xaru smiled, now truly free.

"That's so much better," he said to Nadir. "I can hardly wait to get started."

18

WHEN HE OPENED THE BARN DOOR
the next morning, Parker found Fon-Rahm standing in his corner, arms folded against his chest, exactly as Parker left him. The genie had literally not moved a muscle.

"Good morning, sunshine. I would ask you how you slept, but you don't sleep. I didn't have a great night, myself. My head was killing me. I feel better now, though, thanks for asking."

Fon-Rahm stared straight ahead.

"Okay, then," said Parker. "Here's what's going to happen today. Theo and I promised my aunt Martha that we would run to the store with her to pick up some perennials, whatever they are, and after that, you and I are going to get up to some serious wish-granting. I have been toying with the idea of a helicopter."

Fon-Rahm seemed distracted. He didn't even appear to be listening.

"You with me, buddy?"

Fon-Rahm said, "Something has happened."

"Wow. Here's a command for you: be less cryptic. *What* has happened?"

"I do not know. Something has changed. The balance in the Nexus has shifted."

"Okay, I'll bite. What's a Nexus?"

"It is the force of magic that surrounds Earth. I sense dark waves on the horizon."

"Oh. Well, in that case . . ." said Parker. "No, I still don't care. I'll see you in about a half an hour."

Parker left the barn. His headache returned the second he shut the door behind him.

"Come on, Parker," said Theo. He was waiting with his mother in the driveway in front of a ratty Subaru station wagon.

"I'm coming, I'm coming."

With each step Parker took toward them, however, his headache got worse. By the time he reached the car, he was pressing his palms into his eye sockets to try to relieve the pressure.

"Parker?" asked his aunt Martha. "Is something wrong?"

"No, I just . . . I'll be okay. My head hurts."

"It's probably allergies. People who aren't used to the country get them."

Theo got in the car. Parker opened the door to the backseat and grimaced when he climbed in. His aunt looked him over.

"Maybe you should go inside and lie down for a while."

"But . . ."

"Go, Parker. Theo? Why don't you stay with your cousin? There's some allergy medicine in the bathroom."

Theo grumbled and got out of the car with Parker. As soon as Aunt Martha drove off, Parker collapsed onto the driveway.

"Jeez, Parker, are you okay?"

"The barn," Parker said.

Theo helped Parker to his feet. As they neared the barn, Parker's headache vanished. They swung open the barn door to find Fon-Rahm rising from the ground, recovering from a headache of his own.

The genie looked at Parker.

"You, as well?" he asked.

A half an hour later, Parker, Theo, Reese, and Fon-Rahm were standing under the uprights in the visitors end zone of the Robert Frost Junior High School football field. It was set behind the school, hemmed in on one side by hills. It was also deserted on a Sunday morning, which made it perfect for an experiment like this one.

"I don't know, guys," Reese said, scrolling through a Web site on her phone. "I can't find anything anywhere about genies and their masters being attached by the head."

Parker and Theo stared blankly at her. Boys, thought Reese. Really.

"You two didn't even consider Wikipedia?"

"I do not know what knowledge this Wikipedia contains, but the spell that binds me to Parker has clearly also created some kind of a tether between us." Fon-Rahm turned to Parker. "My suggestion is that you walk down this shorn meadow...."

"It's a football field," said Theo.

"This football field, then, until the pain forces you to stop. That way at least we will know how far apart we are permitted to go."

"That's not a bad idea, Rommy," Parker said. "But, of course, losers walk."

Parker pointed to the other end zone. Fon-Rahm rose off the turf and began to float slowly down the field. Reese counted off the yards as he went.

"Ten. Twenty."

"My head already hurts," said Parker.

"Thirty. Maybe he should slow down a little."

Parker rubbed his temples.

"Wow. Yeah, it's getting much worse."

"Should we stop?" asked Theo.

Parker said, "Uh-uh. We have to know."

The pain was obviously getting very bad for Parker. He clenched his eyes shut and began to sweat.

"Forty. Fifty."

"Okay. That's enough," Theo said.

"Sixty."

Reese was starting to sound as nervous as Theo.

Parker fell to his knees. In the distance, Fon-Rahm tripped out of the sky and landed on the grass. The genie struggled to his feet and continued on foot, slowly and in great pain.

"Seventy."

"That's it," said Theo. "Call him back!"

Parker gritted his teeth.

"Just a little bit farther..."

"Seventy-five."

Reese sounded more than a little panicked. Fon-Rahm began to weave. He was continuing on willpower alone.

Parker dropped to all fours. Theo ran to his cousin. By the time he got to him, blood was running from Parker's nose and ears.

"Fon-Rahm!" Theo screamed. "Come back!"

He yelled to Reese.

"Make him come back!"

The genie was no longer moving. He was collapsed eighty yards down the field.

"Reese! Help me with him!"

Reese ran over. She and Theo each grabbed one of Parker's arms. They dragged him as quickly as they could down the field toward Fon-Rahm. As they got closer to the genie, the pain in Parker's head began to go away. They reached Fon-Rahm and they all fell in a heap, spent.

Reese studied the genie's face.

"Fascinating," she said. "What do you think would happen if you got farther apart than that?"

Fon-Rahm and Theo just stared at her.

Parker said, "Let's hope we never have to find out."

19

THE PUCK SLAMMED INTO THE GLASS
right in front of Parker's face. Theo and Reese both flinched, but
Parker kept right on smiling. Fon-Rahm looked like he would
rather be back in his lamp.

"And this is what, exactly?" the genie asked, gesturing to the
ice stretched out in front of them. "Another football field?"

"Close! Good, Rommy!" Parker said, nodding his head
approvingly. "Actually, what this is is a hockey rink. People
put metal blades on their shoes, like so." He held up his new
ice skates. "So they can go really fast, and then they use sticks
to push a hard piece of plastic into a net." He gestured at the
goal.

"Ah. It is a waste of time."

"Nailed it in one," said Reese.

Parker shrugged. "Maybe. What I just said is literally one hundred percent of everything I know about hockey."

The rink was vast, with high ceilings and mainly empty bleachers lining the sides. The floors off the ice were concrete and covered with black rubber mats. The plexiglass topping the barrier that surrounded the rink was cloudy and scratched. It was a classic rink, open since the fifties, and it had been home to countless hockey games, birthday parties, skating lessons, and first dates. There was a snack bar that sold Snickers bars and popcorn, and a pro shop where you could buy gear and get your skates sharpened.

It was so cold inside the building that the kids could see their breath. Fon-Rahm, of course, didn't breathe.

"Then why are we here?" he asked.

Theo said, "Because those jerks are here."

He pointed at the guys finishing up their hockey practice on the ice as they gathered in the center of the rink and took off their helmets. They were the jocks that had tormented Parker on his first day of school. The goalie took off his mask and shook the sweat out of his hair. Then he turned to the bleachers and nodded at a group of bundled-up eighth-grade girls watching from the bleachers. Caitlyn Masters, the redhead Evan had been after all year, turned and whispered something into the ear of a friend. Evan smiled to himself. Caitlyn was having a party later that night and, if he played his cards right, he just might be able to get her alone for a couple of minutes.

"Why, hello, Evan," Parker said.

Theo shook his head. "Let's grab a seat," he told Reese. "This is gonna be good."

The Robert Frost Junior High hockey coach was a patient guy. He liked kids, mostly, and he *really* liked hockey. He had, in fact, briefly played minor league hockey for the rough-and-tumble Syracuse Crunch, but he spent a lot of time on the bench, and he hung up his skates when he realized that if he couldn't start for the Crunch he was probably never going to play left wing for the Canucks. He brooded about it for a few months, but then he met Debbie and bought the place in New Hampshire, and he never looked back. He kept in shape by running laps at the school, he built a deck for the house all by himself, and things had worked out pretty well at the tire shop. Plus, he got to spend his free time teaching kids the game he loved. Not so bad at all. Coach Decker was that rare guy who was completely content with his life. Let the other idiots break their necks trying to get rich and run the rat race. He thought he had it all, and on occasion, he *acted* like he thought he had it all.

He blew his whistle and skated out to his boys. "All right, you doorknobs, let's wrap it up," he said.

Parker finished lacing up his skates and turned to the genie. "Okay. Wait till I give you the signal."

"What is the signal?" Fon-Rahm asked, genuinely confused.

"Um, I'll go like this." Parker shot imaginary guns with both sets of fingers.

"Ah. And where shall I be?"

"Close! The whole effect will be ruined if my head explodes."

"I concede the point."

Parker put on heavy gloves and hobbled to an opening in the wall. He had been on skates once before, with his father, but he was just a little kid then. The only thing he remembered about that whole day was the cup of hot cocoa his dad had bought him after. That was right before his dad took "the job" that turned into "the trial" that turned into "the jail."

Now he placed his left foot gingerly on the ice. It immediately got away from him, and he had to wave his arms in the air to keep from going straight down.

"Poor Parker," said Reese, settling into her seat.

"Yeah," said Theo. "He's not the most coordinated guy in the world."

Parker balanced himself on the wall. "Here we go," he said, and he pushed off.

"Oh, come on. What the"—Coach Decker glared at him, so Evan changed his sentence midstream—"*heck* is this jerk doing?"

The other guys snickered.

"Hi!" said Parker, slipping on the ice. "Whoops! Sorry!"

"Can I help you?" asked the coach.

"I'm Parker Quarry? I'm here to try out for the team!"

"Are you kidding me?" said Evan.

"All right, guys, just . . . I'll handle this." Coach Decker turned to Parker. "Tryouts were last week. We're already practicing."

"Yeah, but I'm new! I just found out about it."

"I would love to let you try out, really, but it just wouldn't be fair to the other . . ."

"Let him try out!" said Evan.

Coach Decker sighed. "Evan, come on."

"No, he's right! We should give him a shot. You don't know. He might be the next Sid Crosby!"

"More like the next..." Evan's friend searched his brain for a good person to compare Parker to, but he had nothing. "The next *loser*."

"Yeah, um, it's Parker, right?" said the coach. "I don't mean to be harsh, but have you ever played before?"

"Nope. But I was watching you guys, and I have to say, it doesn't look all that tough."

A wise guy. Coach Decker knew the type, and he knew how to deal with it.

"All right. You want to try out, let's do it."

"Great!"

Caitlyn Masters and the other girls in the bleachers laughed as Parker lurched on the ice. He managed to stay upright, but just barely.

The coach touched Evan on his shoulder. "Get in the goal." Evan put his mask on and skated gleefully to his spot. "Parker, I'll tell you what we're going to do." He put his hand on Parker's back, causing another near wipeout, and dropped a puck in front of Parker's feet. "Evan's going to stand in front of the goal, and all you have to do is give this puck a whack with your..." He saw that Parker didn't have a stick. "Coleman! Give Parker your stick."

Coleman handed it over. "Ah, man, it's brand-new. I got it for confirmation."

Parker took the stick and used it as a prop to keep himself standing.

"Hit the puck into the net," said the coach. "That's it. You make three goals, you're on the team. Do you think you can do that?"

"I'll do my best, Coach!"

"All right. Good luck!"

Parker grinned and held out his hands out awkwardly, trying to signal Fon-Rahm, but was stymied by his bulky gloves.

The coach said, "Um, what are you doing?"

Parker scanned the arena in search of Fon-Rahm. "I'm, uh, shooting you with imaginary guns."

"Why?"

"It's, um, it's a signal to . . . for . . ." Parker broke into a cold sweat. The girls in the stands laughed and pointed as he craned his neck looking for his genie. Without Fon-Rahm, Parker was just a moron in for the humiliation of his life. He would never live it down. Where could the genie have gone? Finally, Parker leaned his head back and spotted Fon-Rahm twenty feet in the air directly above him. Parker waved to the genie madly. This caused him to lose his balance for good, and he went down hard on the ice.

"Ouch!" said Theo.

"That's going to leave a bruise," said Reese.

The girls roared, and Evan grinned behind his mask. This was almost too good.

Parker struggled back to his feet, peeled off his gloves, and gave Fon-Rahm the signal just as his legs went out from under him and he felt himself going into what would be an incredibly uncomfortable split.

This time there was no missing it. The genie nodded almost imperceptibly, and Parker's legs stopped moving out. He straightened himself up and slowly put his gloves back on. He grabbed the stick, held it out to gauge its balance, and slapped it down on the ice.

"Okay," he said. "Let's go!"

With that, Parker swung the stick back and drilled a shot bullet-straight at Evan. It came in so fast that Evan, scared, dove out of the way. The puck caught the center of the net and dropped to the ice.

The arena was silent. Then a lone voice came from Caitlyn Masters.

"Holy crap!"

Evan pushed himself to his feet. He grabbed the puck from the net and slapped it back to Parker. "I thought you never played before!"

"Yeah!" said Parker. "But I think I'm getting the hang of it!"

Theo looked over at Reese. She was watching Parker, rapt. "I can really skate, you know," he said, turning red the second the words left his mouth. "I mean, without using magic."

Reese smiled at him. "I'll bet," she said.

Coach Decker motioned to three of his players. "Get in there and play some D." They skated out, ready for Parker's next attempt. Parker looked them over and began to skate in slow, lazy, clockwise circles. Then, when he was good and ready, he broke fast to his right, his skates spitting frost as he deked past one defender after another, finally speeding past the goal and slipping the puck in, untouched, past Evan's reaching pads.

The girls started to cheer, and Parker raised his hands in triumph as he took a graceful victory lap on one leg.

Theo couldn't help but smile at the kid's bravado. Theo himself would never be able to muster that kind of guts.

"All right. Everybody on the ice," said the coach. "Everybody. Whitten, Spinelli, everybody!"

The entire team took to the ice. Parker raised his eyes to Fon-Rahm and broke into a huge smile. So. Much. Fun.

When Coach Decker blew his whistle, guys came in from all sides. With the genie hovering unseen ten feet overhead, Parker glided elegantly down the ice, faking one way and then going another, flipping the puck with amazing dexterity as he literally skated circles around his defenders. He saw two Robert Frost Fightin' Poets coming at him from opposite directions, and put on the brakes so quickly that they ran into each other. He stopped and actually gave the puck away to one of the eighth graders, only to steal it back and leave the kid flat on his butt on the ice. He destroyed an entire team, little by little making his way to the goal. When he got there, he raised his stick for a slap shot. Evan buried his head in his hands, waiting terrified for the shot to blow past him. Instead, Parker tapped the puck with the utmost gentleness, and it slid delicately into the goal.

The jocks deflated. They were beaten—worse, they were *dismantled*—by a seventh grader. From *California*.

Parker skated balletically to the wall. Before he climbed off the ice, Coach Decker grabbed him.

"Where are you going? You made the shots. You're on the team! Parker, I'm telling you, I have been around hockey my entire life, and I have never seen anyone play like you. You're going to be the greatest of all time. Better than Robitaille! Better than Guy Lafleur or Bobby Orr or Espo! Better than *Gretzky*! Evan, get this kid a jersey!"

Evan hung his head and skated for the bench. He wouldn't be going to Caitlyn Masters's party tonight. He might not even be going to school tomorrow.

"No thanks, Coach," said Parker as he joined his giggling friends outside the rink.

"What? Why not?"

Parker shrugged. "I think I might take up basketball."

Theo and Reese laughed out loud as Parker unlaced his skates, but Coach Decker was crestfallen. His life was changed forever. He was no longer content, and he never would be. He had lost the greatest hockey player in history.

20

THE NEXT FEW DAYS WERE THE BEST of Parker's life.

He still had to go to school, sure, and with Fon-Rahm hanging around mopey, unseen, and always within ten or twenty yards, that was a bit of a drag. Still, the genie came in handy. He produced correct test answers with only a whispered wish from Parker's lips. He gave Parker the ability to dunk a basketball in gym, stunning the teacher into a stupored silence. He guided Parker's brush in art class, producing a perfect likeness of the hottest girl in school. For the first time in years, Parker really enjoyed the process of learning.

The best stuff, though, happened after school was done for the day. Parker, Theo, and Reese had a blast coming up with new and increasingly more ridiculous uses for Fon-Rahm's power. They stocked up on all the trendy gadgets they could stuff into their closets without getting caught. They jumped off a bridge a hundred feet over the Merrimack River, using only Fon-Rahm's magic as bungee cords. Parker laughed as his beloved Dodgers crushed the Boston Red Sox 31–0 at Fenway, hitting home run after home run directly into his and Theo's gloves in the stands. They tore through the woods, playing paintball on souped-up Segways. Parker learned Spanish, Italian, Greek, and even won an argument with Reese in Latin. When Theo wished for an entire outfit of Ed Hardy clothes, Reese and Parker laughed so hard they thought they might pass out. They had a never-ending supply of milk shakes and Doritos and tacos without getting sick. The only things holding them back were the parents, aunts, and teachers, who would suspect something was seriously wrong if they didn't keep everything hush-hush, and the constant scowl on Fon-Rahm's face that reminded them that the genie was not sharing in their fun. At all.

Parker, Theo, and Fon-Rahm walked into Theo's house. They had spent the afternoon watching Theo use his new instant guitar-shredding talent to shut up the guy in the guitar store before dropping Reese off and heading home.

"Maybe we should leave him in the barn," Theo said, nodding at the genie.

Parker poured himself a glass of water.

"I'd just as soon keep him close. You never know when we might need him for something."

Theo's dad called to them from the next room. "Theo, Parker, come in here for a minute."

Parker and Theo exchanged looks before walking into the living room. Fon-Rahm stayed by the door.

Uncle Kelsey was sitting in a battered but insanely comfortable old easy chair.

"We have a visitor," he said. "Theo, you remember Professor Ellison."

Professor Ellison sat with her back to Parker and Theo on the couch. She turned to the kids.

"Hello, Theo," she said. "Who's your friend?"

Busted, thought Parker. Busted hard. Busted bad. Busted in new ways he had never even been busted before. Busted, busted, busted.

Uncle Kelsey said, "That's Parker, my wife's sister's boy. He's staying with us for a while."

Professor Ellison smiled. If Parker had expected a rumpled old academic, he couldn't have been more wrong. She was an elegant older woman, maybe sixty years old, with long limbs and expensive clothes. Her eyes were a cold gray that matched her perfectly styled hair. She owned the room. The couch was old and covered with a poorly made quilt, but it might as well have been a chaise longue at a five-star hotel's pool.

"It's nice to have family," she said.

"The professor and I were just talking about security at the university. She was telling me that some things have turned up missing from her office."

"Really?" Parker said. "That's weird."

"What did you say was taken, Professor?"

"I don't know about *taken*," she said. "Let's just say it was misplaced. It's nothing to get too worked up about, anyway. Just a worthless artifact someone dug up a few miles from here."

She stared at the boys.

"A metal canister, about yay big. I don't suppose you lovely boys have seen it floating around, have you?"

Busted busted busted busted busted

Theo stammered. "Us? No. Nope."

"It was a long shot, I admit, but you never know. Sometimes missing objects turn up in the strangest places."

Parker felt himself turning red. When the professor suddenly stood, both he and his cousin jumped.

Professor Ellison shook hands with Uncle Kelsey.

"Thank you, Mr. Merritt. We'll discuss the new locks and so forth at your convenience."

"Whenever you're free."

"Such a charming man." She turned to Theo and Parker. "Theo. It was nice to meet you, Parker."

Parker didn't even realize he was holding his breath until Professor Ellison walked to the door and he let it out.

"Oh, Theo," she said, turning back around. "I almost forgot. You might need this."

The professor reached into the Louis Vuitton bag she carried with her everywhere and handed Theo a piece of paper. It was one of his old science homework assignments. His name was right on top. It must have fallen out of his bag when everything went flying in the professor's office. He got a C on it.

Professor Ellison stared at him. "Study hard, Theo. The world needs more great thinkers."

As she walked past Fon-Rahm on her way out the door, Professor Ellison froze. Impossibly, she knew that something was there. She whirled on Parker and Theo, furious.

"You let him *out*?" she screamed. "Are you insane?"

Parker and Theo turned white.

Uncle Kelsey was confused.

"Um, what?"

Professor Ellison took a deep breath and got herself together. "Sorry. I thought the . . . cat had escaped."

Uncle Kelsey said, "Oh. We don't, uh, have a cat."

"Just as well." She looked at Fon-Rahm. "They're nasty beasts."

She glared at Parker and Theo for a moment before Uncle Kelsey walked her out of the house.

Theo panicked.

"She knows! She knows!"

Parker shrugged with false bravery.

"So what?" He looked to his genie. "There's nothing she can do to us."

Later, back in her office at the university, Professor Ellison dropped her bag on the desk and walked into the back room. She pushed the rack of spears aside, exposing the shimmering wall that had knocked Theo for a loop. She muttered an ancient phrase under her breath and reached out. As she touched the wall, her hands disappeared up to her wrists.

She pulled her hands apart, and the wall parted as if it were a curtain. Behind the wall, floating in midair, were four more metal containers just like the ones that once held Fon–Rahm and Xaru.

Professor Ellison took one of the lamps and turned it over in her hands. She was profoundly worried.

21

PARKER SLID THE MONSTER TRUCK TO a stop.

It was a black-and-silver beast, easily ten feet off the ground. The tires alone were taller than Reese, and the truck had the words SKULL CRUSHER 2 painted on the side. Parker had insisted. He thought that the 2 part was cool because it would make people think that something really disturbing had happened to Skull Crusher 1. This didn't really make a lot of sense. No one else was ever going to see the truck. Since the Porsche incident, Reese and Theo refused to get in any vehicle driven by Parker unless they were positive they wouldn't be seen in public. Hence the Crusher, and the deep backwoods of Cahill.

Reese, Parker, Theo, and Fon-Rahm climbed out of the truck

and jumped to the soggy ground. They were miles from the nearest road, nowhere near anything at all.

Theo said, "Parker, enough. We went hang gliding. We hit the water park. We ate lobster. Can we call it a day, please? My folks will get worried."

"Well, we can't have that," Parker said. "Hey, Rommy, can you give his parents amnesia or something?"

Theo chimed in before Fon-Rahm could answer. "No! I don't want my parents to have amnesia! I'm tired and I want to go home for dinner."

"Could someone please tell me what we're doing in a mud field in the middle of nowhere?" asked Reese.

"Sure," answered Parker. "This is where we're going to put the house."

Theo said, "The house? What house?"

"*Our* house. Right here. Fon-Rahm is going to build us a crib."

"Come on, Parker. Why do we need a house?"

"I want a pool," said Reese. Why not? She worked hard. She got stellar grades. She put up with her mother. She deserved a pool.

Parker threw out his arms.

"Yes! *That's* the attitude I'm looking for. We can have a pool. We can have a pool each, if we want, and an arcade and a climbing wall and a bowling alley. And a submarine dock! I can't believe I almost forgot the submarine dock."

"For God's sake, Parker, what are you going to do with a submarine in the middle of the woods?" Theo asked.

"I don't know. We'll build a canal or something to the ocean. A tributary. It'll be amazing."

Theo sulked. "Well, it sounds stupid."

While Theo and Parker bickered, Fon-Rahm scanned the skies with a worried expression.

"Stop," he said.

Parker ignored him. "Okay, forget the submarine, Theo. Put the submarine out of your mind and just think about the house. It'll be our place. We'll make the rules. No one will be able to tell us what to do."

"Stop," Fon-Rahm said.

"We'll get a bunch of four-wheelers. You *like* four-wheelers." Parker could see Theo wavering. He *did* like four-wheelers. Then Parker added, "We can bring girls out here."

To Reese's surprise, this hit hard. She had no interest, really, in Parker or in Theo. They had been having fun, sure, and maybe you could say they were friends, but it's not like there were any romantic feelings, at least not on her end. So why did this disappoint her so much?

Fon-Rahm exploded with anger. "Stop!" he screamed.

The kids stared at Fon-Rahm.

"I sense something nearby," the genie said. "Something that disturbs the Nexus. I can feel it moving."

Parker dismissed him.

"Get over it, Fon-Rahm. You're always feeling something. I think you should get used to the idea that you're my servant, and the only thing happening is me getting everything I ever wanted."

Theo blanched. "Jeez, Parker. That's a little harsh, don't you think?"

"Stay out of it, Theo. I'm the one who found him, not you."

"It's getting closer," said Fon-Rahm.

Theo got in his cousin's face. "You know what, Parker? I'm getting pretty sick of this. How come we always have to do what you want to do? We're *all* in trouble if we get caught."

"Are you kidding me? If it had been up to you, none of this would even be happening. We would have taken the lamp back to the college."

"Yeah, yeah, you're great and everybody else is an idiot."

"Not everybody, pal; just you. And if you don't want to hang out with Rommy and me, you don't have to." He turned to Reese and added, "Either of you."

Parker knew he had gone too far. He knew he was being a jerk, but once he got started, he found it hard to stop. Theo didn't deserve his abuse and neither did Reese. They were his only friends.

He opened his mouth to apologize, but Reese shushed him. She was far more interested in what Fon-Rahm had to say.

"Wait. What's getting closer? What's coming?"

"Xaru," Fon-Rahm said.

Theo walked away from his cousin. "Xaru?" he said. "What's a Xaru?"

Instead of answering Theo, Fon-Rahm threw his arms into the air. A blue crackle of electricity crawled from his shoulders to his wrists and burst off his fingertips, creating a shimmering, domed force field around himself, Reese, Parker, and Theo that sealed just as the ground around them exploded. The Skull Crusher 2 was blown end over end like a plastic toy. When the rain of trees, debris, and hot rock finally hit the dirt, the area under the dome was the only thing for half a mile in any direction left unscorched. The air reeked of sulfur and charred wood.

The kids huddled together in fear as the force field dissolved. They all followed Fon-Rahm's gaze into the sky.

Xaru, majestic and malevolent in his billowing red robes, floated down until he was just a few feet off the ground, directly in front of Fon-Rahm.

"Hello, brother," he leered, smoke all around him. "It's been ages."

22

WITHOUT A SECOND'S HESITATION, FON-
Rahm sent a bolt of blue lightning at Xaru.

The blast caught the other genie square in the chest and threw
him half a mile. Xaru hit the ground feetfirst and launched himself full-strength into Fon-Rahm. Xaru snatched Fon-Rahm
from the ground and the two genies smashed into the twisted
remains of the truck.

"Now isn't that just like you, to lash out at me before you've
even heard what I came to say," said Xaru.

"I can guess what you came to say, and my answer is the same
as it always was. No!"

Fon-Rahm freed himself from Xaru's bear hug and punched
him in the face. If Xaru was fazed, he didn't show it.

"So stubborn," he said. "After all the time you've had to reflect,

I thought that perhaps you might finally be convinced of the wisdom of my proposition. This new world could be ours, Fon-Rahm! Join me!"

"Never!"

Fon-Rahm took to the sky and set his hands to unleash another storm of lightning.

Parker screamed, "Stop!"

Fon-Rahm halted in midair. Theo and Reese were huddled together on the ground, but Parker stood defiant and unafraid.

"There are *more* of you?" he asked Fon-Rahm.

"You must stay away from this!" Fon-Rahm said. "It is not your concern!"

Parker looked at the barren waste surrounding them. "Anything you do is my concern. I command you to protect us!"

Fon-Rahm had no choice. He directed his energy away from Xaru to create another force field over the kids.

Xaru floated up to him, sadly shaking his head. "You are Fon-Rahm, first of the Jinn, and you take orders from a human child? You and I are gods! We are legends made real!"

Fon-Rahm put himself between Xaru and Parker.

"I do what I am compelled to do," he said.

"You and I have always viewed the rules differently, brother."

Parker said, "Take us out of here, Fon-Rahm! Now!"

Xaru grabbed Fon-Rahm's arm.

"Let me kill this little pest, Fon-Rahm. Then, if you refuse to join me, it will at least be your own decision. I mean, really. It's just too sad."

"I cannot allow you to do that. Stand aside."

Xaru threw up his hands in frustration.

"After what they put you through! After they shoved you in a box and left you to rot for eternity, you still believe that humans are worth saving! You still believe that humans are our betters!" Xaru sighed. "You're as deluded as you ever were."

Fire erupted from Xaru's eyes and went at Fon-Rahm like a hellish blowtorch. Fon-Rahm struggled against it, unable to shield himself or turn away. He was using all of his strength to protect Parker and his friends.

Reese couldn't take it any longer. "He's killing Fon-Rahm! Do something, Parker!"

Parker thought for a moment.

"Fon-Rahm!" he said. "I command you to kick Xaru's ass!"

"Thank you," the genie said.

The force field blinked out of existence as Fon-Rahm turned his energy to fighting Xaru. He pulled back his mighty fist and punched Xaru with enough force to turn a building into rubble. Xaru struck back with a wicked slash to Fon-Rahm's face. The trees shook as the two beings traded blows.

Xaru smiled, enjoying himself immensely. He was, literally, born to fight.

"That's more like it, Fon-Rahm! Your little vacation did wonders for you!"

"Neither of us can win, Xaru. We are too evenly matched. This will always be true."

"Oh, I don't know about that, brother. *Always* is an awfully long time."

Xaru swung up his leg and landed a kick that sent Fon-Rahm flying into the distance.

Reese looked at Parker and gasped. "Parker!"

He was lying on the ground, clutching his head. The sudden distance from Fon-Rahm had brought on massive pain.

In the skies, Xaru reached his genie brother. He saw that Fon-Rahm was struggling and quickly determined what had happened.

"Well, look at that. You're chained to this mortal. Yet another gift from the humans. I must say that is unfortunate."

With all the energy it would take a human to pull up a dandelion, Xaru uprooted a maple tree. He swung it at Fon-Rahm like a Louisville Slugger and connected, knocking Fon-Rahm even farther away from Parker.

Parker's nose gushed blood. Reese cradled his head while Theo watched the action in the air, silently wishing that none of this had ever happened.

Weakened to the point of immobility, Fon-Rahm hung limp in the air, gently turning in the wind. Xaru dropped the tree and approached him with what seemed to be genuine pity.

"I hate to see you like this. I really do. You were the first of us, and I admit that I have always felt a certain . . . tenderness for you." He reached out his hand and gently brushed a speck of dirt off Fon-Rahm's face.

"Then again," he said, "I really, really like to kill things."

With that, Xaru wrapped his hands around Fon-Rahm's throat. As he sucked the life force out of his older brother, Fon-Rahm became more and more gaunt. The genie was dying.

Xaru let a smile of deep satisfaction appear on his lips.

"Sleep well, brother."

He was startled by a voice from below.

"Now, really, you two. Haven't we been through this all before?"

The smile disappeared from Xaru's face as he looked down to see Professor Ellison in the clearing, standing next to a silver BMW SUV.

23

XARU SPIT AT PROFESSOR ELLISON. "You!" he hissed. "Still you live?"

"Still I live," said the professor, serene in the face of the magical destruction that surrounded her.

"Who's that?" asked Reese.

"Um," said Theo. "This lady that works with my dad?"

"I wondered how long it would take one of you to get out," Professor Ellison said, nonchalantly opening the rear door of her truck. "Your capture was a bit of a rush job, I admit, but under the circumstances, I would say I did fairly well."

Xaru kept his hands around Fon-Rahm's neck.

"Do your worst, witch," he sneered. "Without your little metal boxes, you're as helpless as a child."

"Who said I was without them?"

With a flourish, the professor pulled off the sheet covering the cargo bay of her SUV, revealing two metal cylinders just like the ones that once imprisoned Xaru and Fon-Rahm.

Beads of sweat appeared on Xaru's forehead. He released Fon-Rahm as Professor Ellison started to chant in an ancient language of arcane magic. Reese and Theo watched, stunned, as dirt and leaves on the clearing floor kicked up and began to whirl around Professor Ellison. She was creating a tornado that grew steadily in strength and size while her spell took shape.

The containers popped open, ready for new tenants.

"No," said Xaru. "No! Not now! Not again!"

Xaru struggled as the new wind became a vortex pulling him and Fon-Rahm down toward the lamps. Using all of his strength, Xaru managed to break free of the fledgling spell before he was sucked in.

He snarled at Fon-Rahm. "We'll have to continue this another time, brother."

Xaru hurled himself up and away, and in seconds he was gone from sight.

"He's gone!" said Theo, as relieved as he had ever been in his life. He yelled to Professor Ellison to be heard over the gale-force winds. "You can stop now! Xaru's gone!"

"I can see that, dear boy, but that's no reason for me to leave here empty-handed."

She continued her spell, and Theo realized that Fon-Rahm was just floating there in the sky, ripe for the picking. Professor Ellison's chanting grew louder and more intense. The wind was now a cyclone that tore through the clearing, throwing rocks, dirt, and entire trees out of its way as if they were made of paper.

Fon-Rahm hovered in the air, his arms and legs dangling helplessly. He began to circle over Professor Ellison as her spell sucked him in. He whipped around, faster and faster the lower he got.

As Fon-Rahm was pulled closer, Parker sat upright, suddenly recovered. He brushed the blood from his nose and looked up to see a revived Fon-Rahm clawing powerlessly at the sky.

"Parker! She's trying to take him away!" cried Reese.

Parker shook the cobwebs out of his head and stood on legs made of rubber. He sized up the situation and came up with what he considered to be a fairly sophisticated plan of action. He ran at Professor Ellison and tackled her to the ground.

When Professor Ellison's chanting stopped, the tornado stopped with it. The air became abruptly still, and Reese and Theo stopped gawking long enough to shield their heads from falling forest debris.

Parker tried to pin Professor Ellison down. "Will you two stop staring and help me, please?"

Reese and Theo snapped out of their stupor and pounced on the professor. Parker and Theo each held one of her arms while Reese wrapped up her feet and held on for dear life as Ellison kicked furiously.

"Haven't you imbeciles done enough?" she said. "Get off me!"

"Hey, Fon-Rahm, we could use a hand over here!" Parker said.

Fon-Rahm landed next to the tangle of bodies in a heap, exhausted from fighting Ellison's spell and his battle with Xaru.

"Let her be," he said, staggering to his feet.

Parker doubled his efforts as Professor Ellison thrashed. "She was trying to put you back in a lamp!"

"She has her reasons. Let her go."

Parker released Professor Ellison's arm. She kicked Reese away, shoved Theo off her, and stood.

"These pants are ruined, thank you," she said, brushing angrily at her legs. "And these shoes cost more than your father makes in a month."

Parker glared at her.

"All right," he said. "Let's hear it. What's your beef with Fon-Rahm?"

"My beef? With Fon-Rahm. Lovely." She stared down her nose at Parker. "I would tell you, but the day I feel the need to explain myself to you is the day that monkeys fly out of my ears."

Parker shrugged.

"Fon-Rahm, I command you to make monkeys fly out of the professor's ears."

Reese shook her head at Fon-Rahm. The ancient genie was many things, but a guy who got jokes was not one of them.

"Fine," said Professor Ellison. "I'll explain it to you. I'm not saying that you're capable of understanding it, but I can try. Come here."

Parker and his friends hesitated.

"Come here, you stupid children. I'm not going to hurt you."

Parker, Reese, and Theo approached her as warily as if she was a really nasty-looking spider. Professor Ellison waved a hand over them, said two words that didn't sound like they made any sense, and closed her hand into a fist.

Instantly, the knowledge of how Vesiroth created the Jinn was shot into their heads. They saw the desert pit lined with jade and smelled the brimstone burning. They felt Vesiroth's loss when his family was killed, and the triumph he felt when Fon-Rahm stepped forth out of the smoke. They listened as Tarinn's pleas to Vesiroth went unheeded. They were there as Fon-Rahm refused to obey his creator, and they witnessed firsthand the birth of Xaru. They saw Xaru find the Elders' deadly spell and begin to create genies of his own. They stood on a rooftop and watched as Fon-Rahm and Xaru battled over Mesopotamia three thousand years ago. They felt the heat of Xaru's fire and heard the clap of Fon-Rahm's thunder as the genies fought to a standstill in the sky. They knew about the Nexus, and they could feel its power all around them.

They saw the sultan, a man of immense power, reduced to begging Tarinn to save what was left of his city. They were in the room when Tarinn agreed, with the sole condition that the genies would be given to her for safekeeping. They were there as Tarinn climbed the tallest building in the city and used a rare alignment of the planets to trap the Jinn in thirteen metal canisters engraved with magic. They watched as the sultan betrayed Tarinn, throwing her in a dungeon while he sent his men to scatter the lamps across the globe, to mountains in Europe, deserts in Asia, jungles in the Amazon, and a forest in what would one day be called New Hampshire.

The greatest power the world has ever known was divided and spread across the world, never to be collected again. It had simply vanished.

Professor Ellison unclenched her fist. Parker, Reese, and Theo, freed from her spell, fell to the ground. The onrush of new information was almost too much for their minds to bear.

"What happened?" asked Theo.

"We got schooled," Reese answered, rubbing her butt. She had fallen pretty hard.

"There are so many of them," said Parker. "I didn't realize there were so many."

The professor rolled her eyes. "Of course you didn't. You're a child. You're not even a very smart child."

"Well, that's just rude," Parker said.

Theo confronted the professor. "How did you do that to us?"

"It was a simple spell. Anyone with a pulse could master it."

"But why do you know spells? And how come you know about all that stuff, anyway?"

"She knows," said Fon-Rahm, "because she was there."

"You were Vesiroth's apprentice," Parker said. "You trapped all of the genies to start out with. You're Tarinn."

"I'm using Ellison these days. It's simple to spell and it's easy to forget."

Reese couldn't believe it. "Come on. That would mean you're over three thousand years old!"

"Careful," said Professor Ellison.

"This can't be right," said Theo. "It's impossible."

"Really, Theo? After everything that happened to us this week you still think things are impossible?" Parker looked at Professor Ellison with newfound respect. "You're a *wizard*."

"Enchantress, conjurer, necromancer, spellbinder, thaumaturge, alchemist. I have always thought 'sorceress' has a certain panache."

"How did you get out of the dungeons?" asked Reese.

The professor shrugged. "Time moves differently for some of us. Vesiroth had taught me many things, some without even knowing it. One was the secret to a very, very, very long life. I outlived the sultan, and his son, and *his* son, and eventually, I outlived the sultanate itself. There were mobs and lots of exciting riots. The dungeons were cleared and I was free to go on my merry way. I have been hunting for the lamps ever since."

"What happened to Vesiroth?" asked Parker.

"I wish I knew," she said wistfully. Her feelings for Vesiroth were . . . complicated. "I have lived a long time, and I have faced many threats, but the only thing that keeps me up at night is the idea that he's out there somewhere, frozen but alive, waiting to be free once again."

Professor Ellison allowed herself a moment to remember, before she turned her attention back to the matter at hand.

"Now please, children, stand aside." Professor Ellison bored her eyes into the genie in the black suit. "Fon-Rahm and I have unfinished business."

"That we do," the genie said, pointing into the distance. "But perhaps we could discuss it later."

The kids looked where Fon-Rahm was pointing and saw four Jeeps explode through the trees. They were filled with men in black suits carrying machine guns, and they were headed straight for them.

24

"YOU HAVE GOT TO BE KIDDING ME,"
said Theo.

"It has to be those guys that tried to kill us before," said Parker.
"Stop them, Fon-Rahm!"

Fon-Rahm shook his head, spent. "I cannot. I am...too
weak." It was true. After fighting off Professor Ellison's attack,
Fon-Rahm could barely stand. It would take time before the
Nexus would re-energize him.

The professor calmly assessed the situation.

"Get in my car," she sighed. "If you want to live."

The kids exchanged looks.

"What about Fon-Rahm?" asked Parker.

"Fon-Rahm, too." Professor Ellison looked at the genie with
disgust. "I want to keep an eye on him."

Seconds later, they were ripping through the woods in Professor Ellison's BMW. Theo tried to keep his head as low as possible, but the BMW was bouncing around like crazy. It was all he could do to stay off Parker and Reese. Strange, he thought. Just last week his biggest worry was not making the football team. Now he was riding in a car with a genie and a three-thousand-year-old sorceress while men in Jeeps shot at him with machine guns. Professor Ellison and Fon-Rahm, in the front seat, didn't seem overly concerned. They had seen worse, probably, Theo thought.

Definitely.

Ellison gave Fon-Rahm the once-over. "What happened to the robes?" she asked.

"I wear these clothes at my young master's request."

"Always a stickler for the rules. The suit makes you look like a bouncer."

Reese popped her head up long enough to see that one of the Jeeps was right alongside of them.

"They're coming!"

Professor Ellison expertly jerked the wheel. The BMW rammed into the Jeep, which swerved madly before recovering and rejoining the chase.

The first bullets came. They were way off their mark, but the point was made. Ellison stepped on the gas.

More gunfire erupted. This time, a bullet shattered the rear window. Reese shrieked. Professor Ellison made a series of high-speed turns, weaving in between the trees. Metal howled as she clipped off branches with the truck's fender and roof. Professor Ellison let the Jeep come closer, and then aimed the BMW straight at a massive pine tree. She waited until the Jeep was directly behind her, and at the last second, made a brutal turn to the right that took the SUV up on two wheels. The Jeep didn't make the turn and crashed full speed into the tree. It made a gruesome noise. The BMW thudded back on all four wheels and kept going. There were three Jeeps left.

Two Jeeps pulled even with the BMW, one on either side. Professor Ellison slowed the SUV to match their speed and rolled down the rear windows. Theo, Reese, and Parker were terrified. They could see scowling men aiming their guns right at them.

"Heads down, please," said Professor Ellison.

The kids ducked just in time. The Jeeps both fired a steady stream of bullets that shredded through the BMW, went over the kids' heads, and exited straight through the other side. The men in the Jeeps cut each other to ribbons with their own gunfire. Both Jeeps peeled off and crashed, out of the chase for good.

The men in the last Jeep fired at them. They were getting close.

"Take the wheel, please," Professor Ellison told Parker.

Parker wriggled his way into the front seat and took over the BMW as Professor Ellison opened the sunroof. She grabbed her Louis Vuitton bag and stood with her body half out of the SUV.

"Um, Professor Ellison?" said Reese.

The professor was not taking questions. As the men in the Jeep tried to get a bead on her, she calmly rooted through her bag and came up with a small marble-and-glass amulet shaped like a pyramid. She closed her eyes, held the object up, and said a few words under her breath. When she was done, she opened her eyes and pointed the amulet at the Jeep.

One of the men in the Jeep was pointing a rocket launcher directly back at her.

Just as the man in the Jeep fired the rocket, the professor's magic took effect. The Jeep stopped dead in its track and lurched straight into the air. When it came down, the Jeep hit the ground and exploded into flames.

The rocket spiraled wildly into the sky, its trajectory ruined. Everyone in the BMW watched it, hoping it wasn't what they all feared. When it righted itself and plummeted directly at them, their hopes were broken.

"Heat seeker!" cried Theo. He was the veteran of a thousand video game wars, and he knew what he was talking about.

"It will miss us," said Professor Ellison as she climbed back into the truck. She shoved Parker to the backseat so she could take back control of the speeding BMW.

Reese said, "I'm not so sure."

The professor swung the BMW around, trying to shake the rocket, but it was no use. The missile picked up their heat and streaked right at them. Professor Ellison spun the SUV around again and headed back toward the burning Jeep.

The man who had fired the rocket stumbled out of the wreckage, bruised, scorched, but still alive. As the BMW sped at him, he fired his handgun into its windshield. Neither the professor nor Fon-Rahm paid him any attention. The man ran out of ammunition and dropped his gun. He was sure the SUV was going to plow into him, so he hid his head in his hands. When at the last second the BMW turned away, he peeked out. Xaru be praised, he had survived!

Then he saw his own missile blasting toward the blazing Jeep, and he screamed. The missile exploded, leaving a rain of metal, burning dirt, and a crater behind.

25

PROFESSOR ELLISON SLID WHAT WAS
left of the SUV to a halt, and everyone got out. Reese gaped at
the hole where the Jeep had once been.

"You killed them," she said. "You killed all of them."

"Would you rather that they had killed us?" Professor Ellison
asked.

"I would rather that no one got killed at all."

Ellison shrugged. "They're prepared to die," she said. "They
call themselves the Path. They're the descendants of a very old
and very disciplined religious order that worships the Jinn. It's
impressive, really. They recruit members from around the world
to renounce their nations and pledge their lives to bring about
genie rule."

"They *want* to be ruled by genies?" asked Reese.

"Some people are more comfortable in chains."

"The Path are fanatics and they will stop at nothing to ensure that Xaru succeeds in his mission to control the world," said Fon-Rahm. "They are after the lamps."

"They must have found a way around the tether," Professor Ellison mused. "How do you like that, by the way? It's just a little something extra I threw in when I trapped you, as a precaution."

"I don't understand," said Parker. "If you think the genies are such a threat, why mess around with lamps? Why not just destroy them?"

Fon-Rahm answered, "If one of the Jinn is destroyed, his power will return to Vesiroth. The wizard must not live again. This time he might succeed, and mankind would forever be under Vesiroth's thumb."

"It might be worth it, for a world without war," said Theo.

Reese shook her head. "Yeah, if you want an evil wizard making all your decisions for you."

"Xaru was trying to kill Fon-Rahm. Isn't he worried about Vesiroth?" asked Parker.

Fon-Rahm frowned. "I do not believe he cares. My brother is an embodiment of chaos. Where he goes, madness follows."

"And that's why I have to find the lamps before the Path does," said the professor. "They have already unearthed Xaru. Who knows what else they've found?"

"Okay, fine," said Parker. "There are twelve evil genies out there. So go get 'em. I don't see why you have a problem with Fon-Rahm. He's on our side."

"He shouldn't even exist!"

Professor Ellison realized she was yelling and made an effort to get herself under control. "He isn't human. He doesn't feel the things that we feel. He has no emotions. He doesn't understand what it's like to be a human being. He might talk a good game, but don't be fooled. Fon-Rahm is a weapon. He is too powerful to be free, and he is not to be trusted."

She looked at the genie with nothing but contempt. "He is simply a spell that got out of hand."

Fon-Rahm stared back at her. "I will fight you if I must. This time, I warn you, I will be prepared."

Smoke began to pool around his eyes. He was now rested and ready to go. Professor Ellison stared him down. It was a standoff, and it was getting very tense.

Parker stepped between them.

"Wait! Wait! You both agree that the genies are a threat, right?"

"The others must be trapped, I agree," said Fon-Rahm.

"You *all* must be trapped," countered the professor.

Parker said, "Then the logical thing for us to do is join forces."

"Us?" Professor Ellison huffed. "I hope you're not under the impression that I need *you* for something."

"Yeah, okay, you might not need me, but you could use Fon-Rahm, and he can only do what I tell him to do. We're a package deal."

"I am doing quite well by myself, actually. Why on earth would you think I need Fon-Rahm?"

"Because Fon-Rahm can tell where the other genies are."

Fon-Rahm looked away.

"He can?" Reese asked. "How?"

Parker turned to the genie. "You can feel them, can't you, Rommy? That's why you knew Xaru was here. I think you even knew when Xaru's lamp was opened. You were talking about a disturbance in the Nexus the first night we stashed you in the barn."

Fon-Rahm let a hint of a smile play across his lips.

"I believed you were not paying attention."

"So," said Reese. "Fon-Rahm is the only one who can sense where all the genies are, and Professor Ellison is the only one who can trap them. It's pretty clear that we'll be stronger and more effective if we work together."

The genie and the professor glared at each other. Neither wanted to be the first to back down.

Fon-Rahm broke the silence. "It's agreed, then? We join together to recapture the other twelve?"

Professor Ellison nodded. "Agreed."

"Ha! Yes!" said Parker. "This is going to be so cool!"

"That's one word for it, I guess," said Theo.

Parker, Reese, and Theo walked back to the BMW. The SUV was dented and Swiss-cheesed with bullet holes. The windows were gone. The roof was barely attached. It took Theo three tries to open one of the back doors. He had to brush broken glass off the seat before he got in.

Professor Ellison and Fon-Rahm lagged behind.

"You realize, of course, that when this is all over I'll be coming for you, dear," she told Fon-Rahm.

Fon-Rahm smiled a grim smile. "I would expect no less," he said.

26

THE ARMY BASE WAS ABANDONED.
The people of Lithuania, poor but resourceful, had stolen anything of value long ago, leaving nothing behind but rusting metal, weeds, and empty cinder-block buildings that were already crumbling.

Nadir sympathized. He had come from nothing himself, and he had no time or patience for those who didn't help themselves, through legal means or not. The world was a cold place. Nadir's strategy was to embrace its cruelty.

Most people would have regarded Nadir's childhood as a horror. He had been orphaned at a young age and left to scrounge for food in the trash cans and back alleys of Munich, alone and unloved. What he couldn't beg, he stole, and by the time he was nine he had progressed from stealing food to lifting wallets, purses, and whatever else he could lay his hands on. He was good, too, nimble-fingered and quick, and with a mean streak that frightened both competition and companionship away. He might have grown up to be a crime boss, or he might have been jailed as a thief, if he hadn't one day innocently walked off from a teeming restaurant with a nondescript black leather briefcase. He had run around the corner and hid behind a wall before opening it, expecting to find money, or something he could sell, but the only thing in the case was a list of names. Some were crossed out in red ink.

Another child would have thrown the list away and gone back to shoplifting and picking pockets. Nadir, however, was intrigued by the list. It was information, and information was often worth more than watches or rings.

He tracked the owner of the case (not difficult for a child who lived on the streets) and found a lean, dead-eyed Colombian man with odd tattoos and a black suit. Nadir offered to give him back the list in exchange for cash.

The owner of the case had an eye for talent and was impressed both with Nadir's skill and his nerve. He didn't give him money, but he gave him something better. He gave him a home.

That man turned out to be the leader of the Path. He became a father figure to Nadir, and the boy worshipped him. He taught Nadir about the Nexus and the Jinn, and he trained him in the dark arts.

Nadir took to his new calling with enthusiasm. He learned the language of the Path and took a new name to show he had broken completely from his old life. When he learned that the collection of names he had stolen was a list of the Path's enemies targeted for assassination, he snuck away and killed one himself.

He was ten years old.

Nadir missed his father figure, sometimes. Sometimes he even regretted killing him, but it was the smart move. Nadir had taken over leadership of the Path himself, and he had never looked back.

Nadir stood inside the deserted hangar with his men and Xaru.

"I should have known Tarinn would still be alive," said Xaru. "That woman is too annoying to die. Still, I suppose a few snags are to be expected. Worlds do not enslave themselves."

Nadir had still not gotten used to the idea of seeing the genie walking among them. For so long, Nadir had dreamed of the day the Jinn were free, and now that it was happening, he felt uneasy. He had been told that the Path was to be rewarded for its centuries of service, and he hoped to sit at the right hand of Xaru's throne. So far, though, Xaru had said nothing about a job well done. He only issued demands and spilled blood.

A lamp had been discovered nearby, and the Path was already in the middle of the ritual. A brother wore the robes and knelt, his hands on the lamp, ready to sacrifice himself for the cause. He tried to be brave, but he was shaking. Badly.

Xaru sniffed. "This time we will be ready for her. And for Fon-Rahm."

The sacrifice finished his words and twisted the ends of the lamp. The lamp burst open, throwing everyone back. There, rising in the smoke and stink, was the genie Yogoth. Although he was one of the first genies that Xaru created, he had none of his older brother's charm or intelligence. Yogoth was a misshapen brute, with four arms and a twisted version of the face Xaru and Fon-Rahm wore.

Yogoth lacked even the ability to speak. He pointed at the kneeling brother and grunted.

The sacrifice, scared out of his mind, scrambled to his feet and tried to run. Xaru raised his arms to stop him, but there was no need for magic. In one fluid motion, Nadir drew a knife and threw it. The man fell dead at Yogoth's feet.

The four-armed genie seemed confused. Where was he? Who were these strange men? Did they mean to harm him?

Xaru approached him carefully, his arms outstretched.

"It's all right, brother. You're safe, now."

Nadir turned his cold blue eyes away as the two genies embraced. He had never understood the concept of affection.

27

FON-RAHM CLEARED OFF THE
workbench and unfurled an antique map. He weighed down the
corners with old tools and a coffee can filled with washers and nuts.

Reese peered over the genie's shoulder.

"Are you sure we should be using this?" she asked. The map
was hand-painted on some kind of cloth, and the writing was in
florid German script. "It looks like it might be valuable."

"Priceless, really," Professor Ellison told her. She was sitting,
her legs crossed primly, on the broken tractor. "Sixteenth century.
One of a kind." She shrugged. "It's all I have with me."

Fon-Rahm pointed to the map.

"They unearthed Xaru here, in Greenland," he said as Parker
and Theo gathered in close. "That means that there are eleven
more of us out there somewhere."

"Seven," said Professor Ellison.

They all looked at her.

"Well, what exactly do you think I have been doing with my time?"

Parker said, "Fon-Rahm won't be able to find the other genies until they're freed. We'll have to wait until somebody digs up another lamp."

"The Path already has," said Fon-Rahm, pointing to a spot that was once part of Russia. "Last night. Here."

Professor Ellison sighed.

"The realignment of the planets is causing the lamps to reveal themselves. Three thousand years have passed without a single one of the Jinn getting loose, and now three have been freed in one week. We have to stop this before it gets completely out of hand."

"Yes. We must go and confront the Path," said Fon-Rahm.

"Go," said Parker.

"Yes."

"To Russia."

"Near Russia, yes."

"I'm into it. I'll go pack."

"Wait. Wait. Wait," Theo said. He couldn't take it any longer. "You guys have got this, right? I mean, you don't need me. I'm not contributing anything."

"Too true," said Professor Ellison.

"I mean, look, guys, it was fun to have a pet genie for a while. It was great, really! I had a lot of fun! But this is *crazy*. It's just too dangerous."

"Oh, come on, Theo," Parker said. "Don't be such a . . ."

"Theo's right."

Parker was surprised Reese agreed with Theo. Reese was a little surprised herself.

She said, "We're way out of our league."

Theo was relieved to learn he wasn't alone. "So you guys can go to Russia or wherever, and Reese and I will stay here. Everybody wins."

"I don't believe you two," said Parker incredulously. "Stay here? Stay here for what? Reese, are you really going to fall behind if you miss one violin lesson?"

"Viola," she said, her eyes locked on the floor of the barn.

"And, Theo, buddy, I know you're trying, but nobody even knows you're here. If you didn't show up at school for a week, who would even miss you?"

Theo flushed red with anger. Before he could say anything, though, Parker continued.

"And me? Please. My own mother shipped me out of town. It's Thanksgiving on Thursday and she's not even coming. As sad as it sounds, you two are the closest things I have to friends at all."

The barn was still.

"Something is happening. And we're right in the middle of it. This is our chance to be a part of something big. Magic. Adventure. Don't you see what this is?"

Parker laid his hand on the map.

"This is *destiny*."

"I'll go," Reese blurted, almost without thinking. How had Parker won her over so quickly? "I mean, I never get to go anywhere, except for my grandparents' house in Maine and that one time the academic decathlon team went to Rhode Island."

Theo threw up his hands.

"Fine. Whatever. Go to Russia. Get burned to death by a genie. Get shot by a guy in a suit. I'm staying."

"That is out of the question," said Fon-Rahm.

Parker said, "Hey, if he doesn't want to come, he doesn't have to come. Let him stay here and keep his parents company. Who cares?"

"The Path will kill him!"

The force in Fon-Rahm's voice shocked the kids. They stayed silent while the genie spoke.

"Theo has been marked. Parker. Reese. All of you. The Path does not stop. They cannot be reasoned with. They will give up their lives to bring about a new age, ruled by the Jinn. They will die without a thought if they believe it will help their cause. And now that they have Xaru to lead them . . ."

He didn't even want to consider the possibilities.

"Theo must come with us. It is the only way I can protect him."

The kids all looked at one another.

"We're stuck with each other," Parker said.

Professor Ellison slid off the tractor seat.

"Well, that's settled. See how nicely everything is turning out?"

"Well, yeah," said Reese. "But there's one little detail I think we might have overlooked."

"What is that?" asked Fon-Rahm.

"I think maybe my mom and dad might notice if I'm in Russia instead of my bedroom."

They all let this problem sink in.

"Fine," sighed the professor. "I'll see what I can do."

An hour later, Reese, Parker, and Theo stood in the living room of Theo's house and stared back at themselves.

"Problem solved," said Professor Ellison.

Ellison had used her magic to create exact duplicates of the kids. The fake Reese, Parker, and Theo looked, acted, and spoke just like the real things.

Reese said, "This is too weird."

Theo walked up to his twin and gave him a little push, thinking his hand might go right through it. It didn't. The fake Theo stumbled, regained his footing, and pushed the real Theo right back.

"What are they?" Theo asked.

"They're you, basically," Professor Ellison answered. "I created them in your own images."

Reese's jaw dropped with newfound respect.

"You can create human life?" she said, awed at the prospect.

"No, I can't create human life. No one can create human life. They're illusions. They were programmed to do whatever you would do in any given situation."

"So, um, Reese Two will go to my classes?"

"She'll go to your classes and argue with your parents and make inane comments with a vacant look on her face, just like you."

"I don't like this," said Fon-Rahm, his arms folded across his chest. "This kind of magic can easily spin out of control."

"Oh, relax," said the professor. "I barely put anything into them. In two weeks they'll vanish back into the Nexus. It will be like they were never here."

Parker circled his double, a grin on his face.

"This is wild. How do we know they'll pass for us?"

The fake Parker's voice dripped with sarcasm. "Yes, how could we be expected to master the subtle intricacies of minds like these?"

Parker nodded his approval.

"I like him."

"We have to leave," said Fon-Rahm. "Now. We must reach the Path before they move again."

Professor Ellison said, "It's taken care of. We leave tonight."

Reese was once again dazzled by the prospect of real magic.

"On a magic carpet, right?"

"No," Professor Ellison said with a look that might be considered amusement. "I have arranged something a tad more comfortable."

28

PARKER, THEO, REESE, AND FON-RAHM
got out of the limo and stepped onto the wet tarmac. They followed Professor Ellison past airport workers carrying fuel and up the stairs that led into a gleaming blue-and-white twin-engined Gulfstream jet.

"Chartered G650," said Parker approvingly. "Fancy."

"It's not chartered, my dear boy. I own it." Professor Ellison shifted her bag. "Anyone who lives more than three thousand years and fails to get rich lacks common sense."

"I've never been on a private plane before," said Reese.

"I've never been on a *plane* before," said Theo. When Reese looked at him, he shrugged. "*My* grandparents live right down the street, and I'm pretty sure I never made the academic decathlon team."

Reese said, "I don't know. You're not so dumb," and Theo practically tripped on the stairs.

Parker didn't know it, but as he was boarding the G650, his mother was wheeling a tattered bag through the very same airport, less than a thousand feet away.

She had flown in from Los Angeles on the cheapest flight she could find, sandwiched between a woman with a tiny yapping dog and an overweight man in sweatpants who had fallen asleep on her shoulder. It was a miserable trip, made even worse by the nervous, gnawing feeling that had settled in her stomach the second she had gotten on the plane. She was in no way sure that Parker would be glad to see her when she arrived. She was going to surprise him for Thanksgiving.

"I still think you should have told him you were coming," Aunt Martha said. She was there to pick her sister up in the rusted Subaru.

Mrs. Quarry was tired from the flight but happy to be on the ground.

"Tell him when? He won't even talk to me on the phone." She shook her head. "You know how he is. Parker never would have forgiven me if I told him I was coming and then something came up and I couldn't. I wanted to wait until I was absolutely positive I could get on that plane."

"Well, he'll be happy to see you, I'm sure. He misses you."

"He's good at hiding it."

She squinted out an airport window and saw the Gulfstream jet. Mrs. Quarry shook her head. Private planes were for a different class of person than she would ever know.

"Must be nice to have money," she said, and then she kept on walking.

The inside of the jet was gorgeous and rich, with soft carpet and polished wood accents. Instead of a million seats jammed together, there were white leather recliners. There was a wide-screen TV and a small vase full of fresh flowers on every table.

Professor Ellison placed her bag beside her and sipped on a martini that was already waiting when she boarded the plane. Theo and Parker ran down the cabin, scoping out seats and pushing buttons.

"It sucks that I can't tell anybody where I'm going," said Reese as she sank into one of the chairs. "This is the most exciting thing that has ever happened to me."

Fon-Rahm nodded gravely. "Yes," he said. "I'm sure it will be . . . exciting for all of us."

He looked out one of the jet's round windows and saw that the flight crew was making their last-minute preparations. He turned away before the plane's copilot stepped onto the stairs. The man had a sinister look in his eye. He also had a curved knife stuck in the waistband of his stolen uniform pants, and orders to kill everyone on board the plane.

29

THE G650 WAS OVER THE ATLANTIC
Ocean, flying smoothly through the night sky. The cabin was
quiet. Theo, Reese, and Professor Ellison slept in their seats. The
only light came from the reading lamp above Parker's seat.

He was too wired to close his eyes, and he was frankly amazed
that anyone could sleep at a time like this. They were in a private
jet, streaking over the ocean, on their way into the unknown! His
mind flashed to the rich kids at his old school and how jealous
they would be if they could see him now, and then he realized
that they were in his past. His future was happening right *now*,
and he was the only one awake to enjoy it.

Well, not the only one. Fon-Rahm sat in a recliner facing him,
and Fon-Rahm never slept.

Parker drummed his fingers on the table and contemplated the covered plate in front of him.

"A cheddar cheeseburger, I think," he said. "Medium rare, please, with fries and a slice of raw onion."

Fon-Rahm waved his hand. When Parker lifted the polished metal cover, the food he requested was magically there. Parker dug in. He held the perfect burger to his mouth and then paused. The genie was staring right at him.

"Are you going to watch me the whole time?"

"If you would like me to look away, I will," said Fon-Rahm. "I confess that I have always found the ritual of eating very curious."

"Yeah, well, some people find junk food very calming."

"I would not know."

"You've never had junk food?"

"I have never had any food."

Parker put the burger down. "Never? Like, at all? No chicken fingers or peanut butter cups or Nerds? Jeez, no wonder you're so tense. Here. Try this."

Parker held up a French fry. Fon-Rahm of the Jinn looked at it with disdain.

"Are you commanding me to eat this?"

"I'm not going to command you to eat French fries. You should *want* to eat French fries."

Fon-Rahm just stared. Parker shook his head and went back to his food. "I eat when I'm nervous. Or bored or happy. It's a miracle I'm not a million pounds. You should see me put it away when I go to see my mom at work. My father's the same way."

Fon-Rahm nodded sagely.

"I have much in common with my father, as well."

Parker stopped eating and looked Fon-Rahm dead in the eyes.

"My dad tricked a bunch of senior citizens into trusting him, and then he stole all of their money. Then he abandoned me and my mom when he got sent to prison. Get this straight. My appetite is the only thing I have in common with him."

Fon-Rahm turned his gaze to the darkness outside the jet's window.

"Why did he steal?"

"What's the difference?"

"There are many reasons for men to do wrong. Was he hungry? Was he desperate?"

Parker thought about this for a moment.

"No. He was doing fine. We were doing fine. I mean, we lived in a little apartment and we didn't have fancy cars or anything, but I didn't care. My dad just . . . He was never happy with what he had. He was always complaining about how he deserved better. He had to be a big shot. He couldn't just . . ."

Fon-Rahm waited patiently, but Parker didn't continue. He realized that he might as well have been talking about himself.

"All men have two sides," Fon-Rahm said. "My father created me in his own image, yet there are things about him I do not understand. I doubt I ever will." He turned back to Parker. "Vesiroth was not always evil. He was once just a man who made a mistake."

Parker mulled that over. Then he held up one of his remaining fries.

"You sure you don't want one?"

Fon-Rahm just sat.

"Xaru's right," said Parker. "You are stubborn."

The genie was trapped. He took the French fry and, with great care, put it in his mouth. The look of disgust on his face vanished as he chewed.

Parker beamed. "Good, right?"

Fon-Rahm scooped up the rest of the fries from Parker's plate. He smeared them in ketchup and shoved them in his mouth.

"Not bad," he said.

And then the first missile streaked past the window.

30

PARKER JUMPED OUT OF HIS SEAT.
"What was that?"

"Trouble," said Fon-Rahm. He rose to get the others, but they were already up and staring out the window.

"That was a missile," said Professor Ellison. "Someone's attacking us."

Reese scanned the sky desperately. "Who? I don't see anyone!"

Then, silhouetted against the full moon, they saw another plane.

"Oh. Oh, wow," said Theo. "That's a MiG-17. It's a Russian fighter jet from the fifties. I have a book about old fighter jets. I have a *couple* of books about old fighter jets."

"It's the Path," Professor Ellison said. "They must have followed us."

The MiG banked and then flew straight at the G650, firing its machine guns.

"Get down!" commanded Fon-Rahm, pushing Parker down to the floor of the cabin. Bullets shredded the wall of the plane, but no one was hit. The Gulfstream banked away and the MiG disappeared back into the clouds.

"A simple flying machine," said Fon-Rahm, gearing up for action. "By your command, I will dispose of it."

"No!" yelled Parker. Everyone in the cabin turned to him, sure he was out of his mind. "No. The Path isn't after *you*. They think Professor Ellison put you back in a lamp. They're just trying to kill *us*."

"So what?" asked Theo. "Either way we're dead!"

Parker blew him off and focused on Fon-Rahm. "You can feel when other genies do magic, right? That's how you knew the Path freed Xaru, and that's how you knew to protect us back in the woods."

"Yes."

"Then that means that Xaru can do the same thing to you. That's how he found you."

"Yes, I suppose so."

Theo blurted, "Parker, who cares? We're under attack here!"

"Look, Fon-Rahm, you haven't done any real magic since you fought Xaru. Nothing big or dramatic, right? Which means that he doesn't know where you are. He thinks you're gone! If he knew you were here, he would be here himself to take you on. If you destroy that jet, he'll feel the burst of power and he'll know you're free and working with the professor. We'll lose the element of surprise."

"Parker's right." The professor was as surprised as anyone to be saying it. "Fon-Rahm should stay out of this. Leave this one to me."

She reached into her bag.

In the cockpit, the pilot was steering the G650 into a cloud bank for cover while trying unsuccessfully to call in a Mayday. He couldn't get a signal at all. Impossible, he thought. The only way the radio wouldn't work is if someone had tampered with it, and the only person that could have done that was the new copilot. The pilot turned to confront him. The last thing he ever saw was the gleam of the copilot's knife as it flashed in the moonlight.

As the professor dug around in her bag for a suitable amulet to destroy the MiG, the G650 suddenly lurched. Everyone in the cabin slid back as the plane headed straight down.

Reese grabbed an armrest to steady herself. "What's happening?"

Then the door to the cockpit burst open and the copilot stepped out, his knife dripping blood. Theo could see the pilot's body slumped over the plane's controls.

"He killed the pilot!" cried Theo.

"Then who's flying the *plane*?" asked Reese. She knew the answer. She just didn't want it to be true. No one was flying the plane.

His knife at the ready, the copilot walked deliberately toward Reese, who suddenly missed her mother. At a time like this, math tutoring and sculpting lessons didn't seem quite so bad.

Fon-Rahm stepped in to intercept the copilot. Without his magic, the genie was no stronger than any human man. "Perhaps," he said, "you would prefer to fight with me."

The copilot slashed at Fon-Rahm but missed. The genie grabbed him. As they fought over the knife, the jet entered a death spiral. Everything in the cabin went flying. Parker snagged onto the door of the cockpit.

"Fon-Rahm, I wish I could fly this plane!" he said. Fon-Rahm paused in his battle with the copilot to nod at him, and Parker felt a stream of information flood into his brain. He learned principles of fluid mechanics, the use of avionics, and the operations of every gauge, button, and lever in a Gulfstream jet in less time than it took him to take a breath.

"Hey, Reese, could you help me out for a second, please?" Parker said as he made his way into the cockpit. Reese didn't have anything better to do besides cowering for her life, so she joined him.

The view out of the plane's windshield was terrifying. The G650 was spinning, plunging lower and lower with every passing second. Parker unbelted the dead pilot's body and pushed it aside before he sat behind the yoke. With new knowledge and skill he flipped switches and checked lights as he leveled out the jet.

"I'm going to need you to watch our altitude and airspeed. These gauges right here," he said. "Reese?"

Reese was staring at the dead pilot.

"Reese. You can do it."

Reese snapped out of it. She stepped over the pilot's body and sat next to Parker.

"Okay, good," said Parker with a determined look on his face. He searched the sky and found the Russian jet. It was heading right at the Gulfstream, its machine guns spitting fire.

"Hang on," said Parker, grinning as he expertly slid the G650 away. "We're going to have a little dogfight."

Parker's maneuver caused havoc in the back of the plane. Fon-Rahm and the copilot, locked in an epic struggle for the knife, smashed into the wall next to Theo. Professor Ellison's bag flew out of her hands. When it landed, its contents were thrown all over the cabin.

The copilot got his knife hand free. He pulled back to stab Fon-Rahm. The genie, for the first time in his existence, felt a flicker of self-doubt.

Theo, thinking fast, groped around for something to hit the copilot with. He came up with a golden statue of a monkey that had fallen out of the professor's bag, and swung it at the copilot's head. The copilot simply ducked out of the way. He sneered at Theo, but then the monkey came to life and sank its metal teeth into the copilot's hand. The copilot let out a yelp and rolled himself and Fon-Rahm away. When Theo dropped the monkey, it hit the floor and became a statue once more.

Making himself useful, Theo helped Professor Ellison gather up the things from her bag. There was a quill pen, a lump of misshapen metal, what looked like a voodoo doll, a dried snake, and an assortment of other amulets, talismans, charms, and trinkets.

"What is all this stuff?"

The professor searched the floor. "Just a few things I've

collected over the years. If you see a small glass globe, please hand it to me."

Theo found the globe under a seat and handed it to the professor.

"Thank you," she said, before throwing it against the wall. The globe shattered with a muted pop, blowing a huge hole in the side of the G650. The plane dipped and oxygen masks dropped from the ceiling. Professor Ellison was ready for it, but Theo scrambled just to hold on. He was almost sucked right out of the plane.

"Are you crazy?" he yelled. "I could have been killed!"

"And what would we have done without you?" She looked out the hole. "Now we have someplace to fight them." She caught Theo's eye. "We need to find the Bow of Qartem."

"What's a Bow of Qartem?"

"It's a bow, like an archery bow, but smaller."

Great, thought Theo, looking at the disaster that the cabin had become. That shouldn't be too hard to find at all.

Despite the danger, or maybe *because* of the danger, Parker felt alive and confident. He compensated for the sudden drop in the cabin's pressure with the ease of a seasoned pilot and craned his neck searching for any sign of the MiG-17. He found it, marked starkly against the night sky. The Russian jet banked high, rolled, and made another pass, firing off two more missiles before diving away.

Reese watched the missiles streak toward the G650.

"Parker?"

"Not yet," Parker said, his nerves made of metal.

"Parker?" Reese was getting very nervous now. The missiles were so close.

"Wait for it."

The missiles were right on them. Reese could read the Russian letters on their fins.

"Parker!" she cried, and, at the last second, Parker screamed "Yee-haw!" pushed the stick down, and rolled the Gulfstream away.

Theo was on all fours, searching for the Bow of Qartem. His eyes were drawn to a small object rolling around. He picked it up and saw that it was a small glass vial sealed with red wax. It held some kind of bright green liquid.

"Did you find the bow?" asked Professor Ellison.

"I don't see any bow," he said, holding the vial up. "But I found this."

The professor saw what Theo had and reached out to him.

"Don't touch that!" she yelled.

And then the plane rolled, Theo, Professor Ellison, Fon-Rahm, and the deadly copilot found themselves shoved onto the ceiling of the G650, and the vial slipped out of Theo's hands.

The missiles shot right by and exploded close enough to shake the Gulfstream. Reese was surprised to find herself gripping on to Parker's arm as hard as she could. She let go.

Parker brought the jet out of its roll and watched the MiG speed up and away.

"He's only got one missile left," he said.

When the Gulfstream righted itself, Theo, Fon-Rahm, the co-pilot, and Professor Ellison thudded to the floor of the cabin. Theo stretched out his hand to catch the vial, but it brushed his fingertips, landed with a crash, and broke. On contact with the air, the green liquid started to bubble.

That's probably not good, thought Theo. He was right. Theo was eye level with the carpet, so he got a great view of the tiny flaming skeletons dressed in armor that rose out of the spilled liquid. He tried to stand up, but fell backward as the skeletons grew in size until they were as tall as professional point guards.

The skeletons looked at Theo, their eye sockets empty but for green flame, and raised their burning swords. Theo screamed and buried his head in his hands. No more baseball. No more go-karts. This was it.

The ghostly warriors didn't kill Theo. Instead, they whirled and charged out the hole in the side of the jet in an ill-fated attack on the MiG. It might have worked, too, except for the fact that they couldn't fly. The flaming skeletons just dropped harmlessly into the ocean below.

Professor Ellison kept looking for the bow. "You might want to be careful," she said. "Those are some of the most powerful talismans in history."

Theo agreed. He also noticed that, on top of everything else, the inside of the G650 was now on fire. He watched as a line of flame sped toward Fon-Rahm and the copilot as they wrestled on the floor, locked in their fight to the death. The copilot smiled and forced Fon-Rahm's head to the ground. The fire was racing right toward them.

"Uh-oh."

Parker tugged at the yoke. Something was wrong with the controls. The plane was not responding.

"I don't mean to alarm you," he said, looking out Reese's side window, "but we seem to be having a problem with the starboard wing."

"What kind of problem?" Reese asked.

"Part of it no longer exists."

Reese planted her hands on the glass and looked for herself. Smoke was pouring out of the wing, and a chunk of it was indeed missing. The missiles must have exploded even closer than she had thought.

"Can you still fly the plane?" she said.

"Sure, I can fly it. I can even probably land it, but we're not making any more fancy moves."

He looked out the window and saw the MiG as it looped overhead, preparing to make one more fatal run at the G650.

"It's up to Professor Ellison now."

Theo saw an object by his feet. It was a small bow, maybe four inches long, made out of a knotty twig and strung with a wire of silver. A small metal arrow was already mounted. It looked like a harmless toy.

"Um, I think I found your bow," he told Professor Ellison. He nudged it with his foot, afraid to touch it.

The professor stood at the hole and reached back for the bow.

"Give it to me! Only a sorcerer can wield the Bow of Qartem!"

Theo reached for the bow but stopped. Beyond Professor Ellison he could see the MiG. It was right on them.

"Theo! Throw me the bow!"

Theo couldn't move. He was frozen with fear.

Fon-Rahm knew that they were in trouble. He gathered all the energy he could and flipped the copilot over, pushing his face into the path of the fire. Right before the flames reached the copilot, Fon-Rahm head-butted him and tossed him screaming out of the plane. Fon-Rahm jumped to his feet. Element of surprise or no, he had to act.

"Enough!" he cried. He pushed the professor aside and stood in the middle of the hole, smoke pooling in his eyes, as the MiG headed straight at them in a last-ditch attack. The genie raised his hands, but before he could unleash his terrible magic, the MiG exploded in a burst of bright flame and shattered metal.

Fon-Rahm and Professor Ellison looked behind them to see Theo, holding the Bow of Qartem. It was full-size in his hands, but its arrow was gone. Theo had shot the MiG out of the sky. He lowered the bow, awed at his own ability. When he placed it on the ground, it shrank back down to its toy size.

Professor Ellison attacked the flames with a fire extinguisher. "It appears you have an affinity for magic," she told Theo. "Go figure."

In the cockpit, Parker cleared his throat and grabbed the mic. He grinned at Reese and put on his best Midwestern pilot drawl.

"Ah, attention, passengers. Please fasten your seat belts and put your trays in their upright, locked positions as we make our, ah, final descent. We hope you have had a, ah, pleasant flight, and thank you for flying Parker Air."

Theo collapsed into his seat, as far away from the hole as he could get. Fon-Rahm sat next to Professor Ellison.

"The Path grows more brazen by the hour," he said. "And I will not be able to find Xaru unless he uses his magic. I fear we may be in for a long and fruitless search."

"I know someone who might be able to help us," said the professor.

"Is he human?"

Professor Ellison mulled it over. "Sort of," she said.

31

DESPERATE. THAT'S WHAT ELLISON thought of herself. She could not believe that she had agreed to work alongside the Jinn. She could not believe that her companions were children. It was pathetic. She would only resort to this kind of behavior if she were desperate.

But she couldn't help it. As she led them to their meeting place in one of the seedier parts of Utena, Ellison couldn't stop herself from worrying. Not about the dangers of the city, of course; she could protect herself with any number of simple spells. No, she was worried about herself. Maybe she was slipping. She had *known* that one of the Jinn was hidden near Cahill. That's why she lived there in the first place, so she would be close by. She had *known* that the lamps would start to make themselves more visible. There was nothing she could do about the stars. They were aligned now, just as they had been three thousand years ago, just as they would be in another three thousand years.

Three thousand long years of waiting. Time that moved slowly. Until now.

And she had *known*. She should have been able to do something.

Now two of the Jinn were out, and that meant that two more sources of Vesiroth's power were in play. This was what had made her worry more than anything over the millennia, and now it was happening. No matter how much she had tried, no matter how much she had studied, there was one thing the Nexus refused to divulge: she could never see the future. Ellison could, however, maintain a relatively close control over the present. That is, until the Jinn started to return in number.

All this to say, Professor Ellison was a bit distracted as she walked into one of the least-friendly bars in Lithuania with a genie and three middle-schoolers.

Maksimilian was fat and greasy, with sweat stains under his arms and brown gunk under his fingernails. His eyes were bloodshot. He hadn't shaved in days. He needed a haircut. He needed a shower.

He was at a scarred table in the back of the bar, surrounded by a crowd of cheering, jeering bar patrons, and locked in an epic arm-wrestling match with a shirtless Lithuanian strongman. His fans cheered him on, but Maksimilian was overmatched. His opponent was made entirely of muscle, and it looked like Maks was done for. Just as his arm was going down, however, Maksimilian reached deep inside himself, leaned in, and let out a massive belch into his opponent's face. The he-man, stunned by the evil stench, lost his focus. Maks forced his arm down with a satisfying thud. Victory.

While the strongman complained about what he saw as cheating, Maksimilian stood and acknowledged the cheers of the crowd. He raised one arm to the sky and with the other he drained a glass of cheap vodka.

"He's like a garbage dump brought to life," said Parker, entranced.

Parker, Theo, Reese, Fon-Rahm, and Professor Ellison tried their hardest to fit in. If they weren't standing in the single scariest bar in the world, Parker didn't want to know what was at the top of the list. The place was filled with shady characters with darting eyes and unkind faces. It reeked of body odor and old beer. It was dark and it was nasty. Plus, despite Parker's lies, this was the first time he had ever set foot in a bar. It was maybe not a great place to start.

"He may not look like much now, but Maksimilian was once one of the most powerful magicians alive," Professor Ellison said. "There is not much that happens in this part of the world without him knowing about it."

"Um, do you think it would be okay if I waited outside?" asked Reese as she took a step behind Fon-Rahm. There was a strange man leering at her.

Theo shifted the weight of the bag the professor had given him when they got off the plane. It contained two empty metal canisters.

"I would rather be with everybody in here than outside alone," he said. Reese weighed her options and decided he was right.

When Maksimilian caught sight of Professor Ellison, he broke into a wide grin that showed off one black tooth. "Julia!" he cried, embracing her in a sweaty bear hug. "As beautiful as always."

"It's nice to see you, too, Maks. Keeping busy, I see."

Maks shrugged. "It keeps me in vodka. There is only one reason you could possibly be here. You have finally come to your senses and accepted my proposal of marriage!"

Reese felt a shudder rack her body.

"Long-distance relationships never work, Maks," said the professor. Parker could have sworn he heard a smile in her voice. This is what a three-thousand-year-old woman is like with old friends, he thought.

"I would like you to meet some friends of mine," she said, pointing to Reese, Parker, and Theo. "These are some children. I forget their names."

Theo rolled his eyes.

"And this . . ." she continued, gesturing to Fon-Rahm.

"Wait. Don't tell me," said Maksimilian, looking Fon-Rahm up and down. "One of the Jinn, isn't he? I never thought I would live long enough to actually see one in the flesh." He peered at Fon-Rahm as if the genie was on display. "Fascinating. He can almost pass, can't he?"

"I would prefer it if you spoke to me directly," said Fon-Rahm.

"Of course, of course," said Maks. Then he turned to the professor. "Touchy, isn't he?"

"We need your help," said Professor Ellison.

"Of course you do! No one ever comes to see me unless they need something. What is it? A rare herb? A map to the hidden treasures of Amenhotep IV? An introduction to some crime boss?" Maks waved his hand. The squalid men that surrounded the area all picked up their drinks and moved to the other side of the bar. "Sit! Sit! Can I get you anything?"

"I'll take a beer," said Parker hopefully.

Everyone ignored him. They all sat. Reese was instantly repulsed by the sticky table.

Professor Ellison said, "We're looking for the Path."

Maks seemed surprised. "Somebody's looking *for* the Path? That's a new one. Usually, people are looking to avoid them."

"Do you know where they are or not?" said Fon-Rahm. His patience was wearing thin. "We have no time for games."

"He's not much on charm, is he?" Maksimilian said, a twinkle in his eye. He poured himself another drink. "I may have heard something about them skulking around. What do you want them for?"

"That is none of your concern," said Fon-Rahm.

"It's my concern if you cause trouble and it comes back to me."

"We're not looking for trouble, Maksimilian," Professor Ellison said. "Just a little information."

"I suppose I owe you, after what happened in Mongolia," the fat magician said.

The professor smiled. "I was too much of a lady to bring it up."

Maksimilian took a dainty sip of vodka. "I have heard—now I don't know this for a fact, mind you, as I have not seen it with my own eyes—but I have heard that some hoodlums who may match the general description of the Path have set up shop nearby. I have also heard that they are not alone."

Parker said, "Xaru is with them."

Maks regarded Parker. "Perhaps. I value my own delicate skin too much to go and make sure."

"Where are they?" asked Fon-Rahm.

"Holed up in a closed museum. It used to be named for Stalin, before the unpleasantness. There's not much left after all the looting, but it's big and it's private. There are worse places to hide."

Professor Ellison rose, and the rest of her party joined her. "Thank you, Maks. I'll consider us even."

Maksimilian kept his seat. "Think about my offer, Julia. None of us is getting any younger. Maybe someday I'll tire of waiting and I'll marry someone else."

"My loss," said Professor Ellison as they walked out of the bar.

Parker looked at the professor with a new sense of who she was. "Julia? Really?" he said.

"Shut up," said Professor Ellison.

32

"THIS IS A MISTAKE," FON-RAHM SAID.

They were hiding in the dark, crouched behind a low wall overlooking the crippled museum. It was a blocky monstrosity without windows or adornment, an ugly building, dingy, run-down, and sad even by Soviet standards. In its prime it would have been unpleasant. Now it was downright depressing.

"The Path is not to be trifled with. We should proceed with patience."

"We should go now," said Parker. "We don't have time for games."

"There is always time for caution."

Professor Ellison said, "The boy is right. We don't even know if they'll be here in the morning, and if they leave we may not be able to follow them. Tonight we can catch them by surprise."

They ducked lower as a Path guard made his rounds. He passed right by their wall and stopped. Reese held her breath, but the guard only shifted his rifle's strap from one shoulder to the other. Then he picked his nose and went on his way.

"He's the only guard on this side," whispered Parker.

Theo checked his watch. "I've been timing him. He goes the same way over and over. He'll be back here in seventy seconds."

"I have something in here that will turn him to ash," said the professor as she dug into her bag. "That way his family can save money on the cremation."

"No! We don't have to kill him," Reese said. "We can create a diversion and sneak past him." She rooted around in her brain for something to justify her idea. "That's what they did in *A Tale of Two Cities*."

"One of these days you'll have to get over your squeamishness, my dear."

"Or maybe you can just stop killing everybody that we meet."

While Reese and the professor argued, the guard made his turn and came back to the wall. Theo picked up a baseball-sized rock, took careful aim, and simply beaned the guy in the head with it. The guard folded like a map.

Parker stared, openmouthed, at his cousin.

"What?" said Theo.

They pried off some boards and made their way in through a side door. As bad as the building was from the outside, the inside was worse. The floor was marble and the walls were stained concrete. A few old paintings still hung at weird angles. Broken statues lay on the floor in pieces. It was dark and scary. It smelled like mildew.

Fon-Rahm pointed the way. "I can sense Xaru and one other. They are this way."

They started to walk through the looted museum.

"I can't help feeling we should be armed," said Theo.

"Guns are for simpletons," the professor said. "And they're unnecessary. All we need to do is get within eyesight. I'll cast one spell to trap the genies and another to"—she glanced over at Reese—"*incapacitate* the Path."

Theo said, "Yeah, well, I would still feel better if one of us had an Uzi."

The professor locked eyes with Theo. "You're not wrong to distrust magic, Theo, but I believe you'll find it's sometimes necessary." Ellison paused. "Perhaps I might even teach you a few things. Better you than"—she glanced at Parker—"someone who lacks self-control. Nothing major, of course, but enough to test the extent of your gifts."

"I'm tested enough already, thanks."

"You should give it some thought. It's not an offer I make lightly, and it may not be repeated."

Professor Ellison walked on. Theo stared at the ground and followed behind her.

They crept down a long, soggy hallway and up a curving flight of stairs. As they passed a water-damaged Renaissance painting of a woman, naked except for a strategically placed bedsheet, Parker did a double take. He went in for a closer look and then turned to Professor Ellison.

"Is that *you?*" he asked incredulously.

"I got around," the professor said with a shrug. Reese grabbed Parker by the arm and pulled him away from the painting.

When they got closer to the museum's center, Fon-Rahm motioned for them to be quiet. They all took cover behind a pile of crates and shattered chunks of concrete. They peeked out and saw that they were perched on the edge of a round walkway that looked over a domed atrium. There were holes in the dome, and two stories down, the legs of what was once a giant statue of a Greek athlete stood atop a crumbling pedestal.

They saw Xaru, pacing as he screamed at his minions.

"Find her! Is that too much to ask?" he fumed. "I recognize that you are lower life-forms, but even for humans you are unconscionably stupid. I would have been better off with camels!"

Fon-Rahm spoke in a whisper. "Good. They are distracted." He turned to Professor Ellison. She was pulling the two empty lamps from Theo's bag. The genie regarded her with mistrust. "I have your word that you will not try to trap me."

"I won't. Not yet, at least."

"Fair enough. Do you need anything before you begin?"

"No," she said, "but you might want to get a mop."

"Why?" asked Parker.

"Because when they realize what I'm up to they may very well wet their pants."

The professor made a few last-minute adjustments to the open containers. Then she stood, her arms wide to the sky, and opened her mouth to start the incantation. Before she could get a single word out, Yogoth materialized out of thin air behind her.

They had walked directly into a trap.

33

"PROFESSOR ELLISON!" REESE SCREAMED.

It didn't do any good. The ugly brute Yogoth grabbed the professor with his four arms. He used one hand to bat away her bag of tricks, and another to cover her mouth so she couldn't speak. Fon-Rahm rushed him, but the drooling genie was faster than he looked. He batted Fon-Rahm over the railing, where he landed heavily at Xaru's feet.

Xaru regarded Fon-Rahm with some amusement. "Bring the witch and the children down to me," he said, and three Path members stepped out of the shadows to seize Parker, Theo, and Reese. Two more Path members took control of Professor Ellison from Yogoth. They were careful to keep one hand clamped over her mouth.

On the ground floor, Fon-Rahm shook off Yogoth's hit and reached for Xaru.

"Oh, Yogoth," called Xaru. The four-armed genie leaped from the rail and landed directly on Fon-Rahm, forcing him to back to the ground. Then he grabbed Fon-Rahm by the legs, swung him in a circle, and let him go. Fon-Rahm was thrown through a wall and into the next room. Yogoth followed him through the hole to finish him off.

Reese squirmed in her captor's arms. She knew that Parker would be in pain. She was right. Parker tried not to show it, but his eyes were watering and his teeth were clenched. His head was on fire.

As Fon-Rahm and Yogoth battled in the other room, the Path members hauled the kids and Professor Ellison down to the atrium. Xaru smiled warmly.

"And now we're all together," he said, gently touching Reese's cheek. Theo put all his strength into breaking his captor's grip, but the thug outweighed him by a hundred pounds. He didn't have a chance.

Xaru shook his head. "Humans. Really. It's all too pathetic." Then he raised his voice so he could be heard over the sounds of the brawl in the next room. "You might as well come out now."

Maksimilian stepped into the atrium. Professor Ellison squirmed in the arms of her abductor and stared knives into him. Maks averted his eyes.

"So we're good now?" he said. "You'll call off the Path?"

Xaru stood directly in front of Professor Ellison, enjoying her anger. "Of course. You may go back to your little life, secure in the knowledge that you are a traitor to your own kind."

Maksimilian turned to leave, desperate to be anywhere else.

"I'm sorry, Julia," he said. "May we meet again in happier times."

Maks put his head down and left the museum. Professor Ellison couldn't do anything besides close her eyes and wish that things were different.

There was a mighty crash, and Yogoth was thrown through the wall and into the atrium. He landed near Xaru, bent iron bars pinning his four arms to his sides.

Fon-Rahm, angry, stepped through the hole in the wall. "This is absurd, Xaru. I can defeat any of our brothers, and you and I could fight for centuries without one of us declaring victory."

"How right you are, Fon-Rahm," said Xaru. "Such a flawed plan seems out of character for me. It's almost as if I were only trying to distract you for a few moments."

"Distract me? Distract me from what?"

Fon-Rahm whipped his head around, but he had figured it out too late. Nadir had been training for this moment for years. He was dressed in a robe passed down through generations and covered with arcane runes. His arms were raised, his mind was focused, and he was chanting an ancient spell. Winds whirled around him.

Fon-Rahm's empty lamp was set in front of him, open and waiting to welcome the genie home.

34

THE WIND TOOK FON-RAHM AND SPUN him around the room like a leaf in a hurricane. The genie bounced off the walls and tried desperately to find something, anything to grab on to. It was no use. He was pulled down and, in a haze of fog and brimstone, sucked back into the lamp. Nadir finished his spell and threw his arms to his side. The lamp sealed itself and began to faintly glow. Fon-Rahm was gone.

Parker fell to his knees. There was no hope now. His captor dragged him back to his feet.

If Xaru felt anything at all, it didn't show. "Good," he said. He turned to his prisoners. "Now, then. Tarinn, my old friend, I am well aware that you have, in your possession, one or two other recovered lamps. I have given some thought as to how I might discover where you're hiding them, and I have decided that torturing you until you tell me is probably the most fun."

One of the minions holding the professor pulled out a knife.

"She would rather die than talk!" said Parker. Easy for him to say, thought Reese. No one was threatening to cut his throat.

"Well, let's see!" said Xaru cheerfully. "Start with her left eye and then take her nose," he instructed the Path member. "After that we'll get creative."

Professor Ellison looked truly scared. The goon with the knife pulled back her hair and held the blade inches from her left eye. She locked her mouth shut. She would never talk.

It was Theo who finally broke. "No! Stop! I know where the lamps are!"

Parker said, "Theo, shut up!"

"*You* shut up! They're going to kill her!"

"They'll kill her if you tell them!"

Theo turned to Xaru. "I'll tell you, if you promise to let us go."

Xaru put his hand over where his heart would be, if he had a heart.

"I promise," he said.

"He's lying! Theo!" said Parker.

Theo shut him out. "She has a secret space in the wall at her office at the university. I saw it. It's a hiding place. I bet the lamps are in there."

Parker deflated like an old balloon. He didn't think Theo would really do it.

"Thank you. Now there is a levelheaded boy." Xaru turned to the professor. "And you keep your entire face."

Parker glared at his cousin. Theo looked at the ground.

Xaru walked over to help Yogoth, who was still struggling on the floor. "Now," Xaru said, easily unbending the iron bars that trapped Yogoth's arms. "Nadir. You and I, along with my dear brother Yogoth, of course, will bring Tarinn back to her home, where she will give us the lamps. No doubt she protected it with some kind of a pesky spell. She was always so clever." He picked up Fon-Rahm's lamp and admired the glow. "A mine in Belarus is set to be collapsed tomorrow. It reaches almost five miles into the earth. The rest of you are to place this lamp gingerly at the bottom. When they destroy the mine, poor Fon-Rahm will be buried under millions of tons of rocks and dirt. Let's see how long it takes him to find his way out of *that*."

He caressed the lamp in a cartoonish display of brotherly love.

"We could have shared the world," he whispered to the lamp. Then he spoke to the Path. "Kill the children. Drop their bodies into the mine, as well. No use stirring up trouble."

"But, you said..." said Theo.

"Start with him," said Xaru, nodding at Theo. "No one likes a snitch."

35

PARKER EYED PROFESSOR ELLISON'S
bag. It was plopped down against a wall, kicked aside and ignored
in all the confusion. He didn't know any of the spells that went
with the doodads inside, but he knew the bag was filled with
powerful stuff. If he could reach it, he thought, he'd find some
kind of magical talisman he could use as a weapon. He would
make the guards tell him where they had taken Fon-Rahm's
lamp, and he would figure out a way to stop Xaru from getting
into the secret hiding place in Professor Ellison's office. He would
save the world from genie domination. He would be a hero to
Theo and Reese. His mom would be sorry she had treated him
so badly. His dad would realize that he had made a huge mistake
in being so selfish and abandoning him.

If he could reach the bag.

But he couldn't. Parker was sitting on the floor with Theo and Reese. Their backs were propped up against the base of the statue, and their feet were stretched out in front of them. Their ankles and wrists were tied with rough, itchy nylon rope and, just to make things a little more uncomfortable for them, they were each gagged with a piece of cloth that smelled like sweat and tasted salty. Parker could no more reach the bag than he could swim the Pacific Ocean with a motorcycle strapped to his back.

Xaru, Yogoth, and Nadir had taken the professor and four or five members of the Path back to New Hampshire. Some of the others grabbed Fon-Rahm's lamp and left for the abandoned mine in Belarus. The goons who remained behind were sitting around an old crate, playing cards in the dim light. They were pretty drunk. They goaded and insulted one another in whatever language it was that they spoke. While they were distracted, Parker used a jagged crack in the marble pedestal to saw at his ropes, but he wasn't getting anywhere. He hoped that they would play cards all night.

One of the Path members threw down his cards in frustration and the others laughed. He had lost the game. He protested, but the others waved him off as they got up and collected their gear. One of the goons slapped Parker's face. He said something funny to his comrades and they laughed and staggered out of the atrium. Parker knew that the man they were leaving behind had lost the game and gained a chore. It was his job to kill Parker, Theo, and Reese.

The remaining minion got unsteadily to his feet and carefully folded a map. It took him three tries to find his pocket. Then he weaved his way over to where the children were tied and unsheathed a dagger from his belt.

Parker felt Theo squirming away beside him. Then the Path member pushed Theo's head back and put his knife to Theo's throat. Theo shut his eyes tight.

"MmmmmMMMmM," said Reese through her gag. "MMm-mmmmMMMm." She had something to say. The Path member ignored her and turned back to Theo, but Reese was insistent.

"MMMmmMMMMmMMMMM!" she said.

Finally, the man with the dagger relented. He leaned over and pulled Reese's gag down.

"Thank you!" said Reese. "That thing was driving me nuts."

The Path member had a quizzical expression on his face as Reese swept his legs out from underneath him with one swift and powerful kick. The dagger flew out of the minion's hand as he fell and smacked his head hard on the marble floor.

Parker followed the path of the dagger as it went up and then came down. He managed to spread his legs just enough so that when the dagger landed tip-down, it clanged off the marble floor instead of imbedding itself in Parker's thigh or someplace even worse.

The Path member was out cold. Parker and Theo looked to Reese, amazed.

"Brazilian jujitsu," she said with a shrug. "My mom made me take a class at the Y."

36

PARKER, REESE, AND THEO FOUND
themselves walking down a desolate country road. It was a beautiful night. The stars were out, and there was a warm breeze blowing. The only noise came from crickets. The whole thing would have been magical, really, if they were back in New Hampshire.

But they weren't.

"Okay," said Reese, shifting Professor Ellison's bag on her arm. "So. We don't have any money, none of us speaks the language, and we have no way to get home. All true. All very real problems. I'm not saying they don't exist. But still. How many American kids even get to come to Lithuania?"

Or Latvia, she thought. She wasn't a hundred percent sure exactly where they were at the moment.

"And not just the tourist sites, either!"

Her attempt to lighten the mood was doomed from the start. They had been walking for hours, and the tension between Theo and Parker was ready to boil over. Parker planted himself in the middle of the road and exploded at his cousin.

"What were you thinking?" he screamed. "Why would you tell them anything? They're trying to enslave the whole human race. Do you really think you can trust them? I mean, we all know that you aren't exactly straight-A material, but are you really that stupid?"

"Parker..." Reese said.

"Yeah, well," said Theo, "I was trying to save all of our lives."

"You betrayed us! You handed the professor to the Path! And plus, also, now they have however-many lamps she had stashed away. Do you realize you might have doomed the whole world?"

Theo stared into his cousin's eyes for a moment. Then, without warning, he hurled himself at Parker and tackled him to the ground. Reese jumped back as the two boys wrestled in the middle of the road.

"Me? Me? I'm the one that doomed the whole world? What about *you*?"

"Parker! Theo! Stop it!" Reese tried to break them up, but they ignored her.

"What *about* me?" said Parker.

"It's your fault Fon-Rahm got captured!" Theo was on top of Parker, as angry as he had ever been in his life. "He warned you! He said to be careful, to plan it all out. But *no*. That's not good enough for Parker Quarry. Why listen to anybody else? There's no fun in that! You have to make all the decisions. It always has to be about you! You don't care about anybody but yourself. It's no wonder your own mother can't stand to be around you!"

Everything came to a halt. Parker stopped fighting back and Theo climbed off him. Parker stayed on his back and looked at the moon.

"You're right," he said.

Theo shook his head and threw up his hands. "I'm sorry, Parker. About what I said about your mother. That was . . . I didn't mean that."

"Well, you're right about the other stuff. Will you help me up, please? Theo?" Theo just glared at him. "Fine." Parker pulled himself up from the road and checked his hands for scrapes. "I should have listened to you and I should have listened to Fon-Rahm. I got cocky. I do that sometimes. I can't do anything about any of that now except apologize and admit I was wrong, and I do. I apologize. I admit I was wrong."

Reese and Theo waited. It was the first time either of them had been on the end of a sincere apology from Parker.

"You're right. It *is* my fault that Fon-Rahm was captured, and it's going to be up to me, or, well, to us, to get him back."

"And how exactly do you plan on doing that?" asked Theo.

"I'm open to ideas."

Reese thought for a moment.

"We have the map we got off the Path," she said. "We have the professor's bag and all of her magic talismans. We have a dagger. We have maybe one or two hours before the sun comes up."

"Right," Parker said. "What we need is some way to intercept the Path before they get to the mine in Belarus."

"Come on, Parker. There's no way we can do that," said Theo.

Parker pointed down the road at a barely manned government roadblock. There was a swing-arm wooden traffic gate painted in fading orange and white. A uniformed guard was sleeping in a chair in what could charitably be called a shack. Parked well behind it was a beaten-down old military truck with a canvas roof.

"It would be a lot easier if we had some kind of a vehicle," Parker said.

37

"SOME GANGBANGERS TAUGHT ME
how to do this in LA," Parker said as he crawled under the truck's
dashboard. After a solid four minutes of bending wires with
nothing to show for it besides bent wire, Parker came up again.

"Okay," he said. "So I didn't know any gangbangers in LA."

Theo rolled his eyes. "Yeah. I kinda figured."

They were being as quiet as they could be, but everything
seemed to make noise. The door of the truck creaked. The seat
groaned. Theo stood outside the truck, watching Parker and
occasionally glancing over to make sure the guard was still asleep
in his shack. Theo might as well have relaxed. Nothing ever
happened at this checkpoint, and the guard had gotten used to a
six-hour nap every night.

"Excuse me," said Reese. Parker moved over so that she could slide under the steering wheel. After a few seconds of tinkering, the truck's engine fired with an impatient rumble.

Parker said, "Let me guess. You took a class at the Y."

"Nope." Reese grinned. "Saw it in a Jason Statham movie."

Parker slid her over and got behind the wheel. He unfolded the map he stole from the Path. Their route was drawn in red pen, and their destination marked with an X.

"All right. So, here's Belarus, and here's us," Parker said. "As far as I can tell, these lines in black are railroads. The Path are planning on taking a train to the mine. If we can cut them off before they get on board, we can steal Fon-Rahm back. We'll have to hurry."

He shut his door. Reese looked for a seat belt, but there wasn't one. She moved over to make room for Theo. Instead of getting into the truck, however, Theo started walking.

"Theo? Where are you going?" asked Parker.

"I'm going home." Theo stopped and turned back to his cousin. "I'm sorry. This stuff is just . . . It's too much for me."

Parker said, "How are you going to get home? We don't even know . . ."

"I'll find a phone. Somebody will have a computer. I'll go to the police. I'll stop at a house. Somebody will help me."

"We can't let you go out there alone!" said Reese.

"Somebody has to save Fon-Rahm. It just can't be me," Theo said. "It'll work out. I'll be okay. Really. I'll be okay."

The two cousins looked at each other for a moment.

Theo said, "So, good luck, I guess. I'll see you when you get back. I'll save you some Thanksgiving turkey."

"Yeah," said Parker. "We'll see you then."

Parker put the big truck in gear, gave it some gas, and looped around the guard shack. He tore through the swing arm over the road, startling the guard awake. The guard ran after the truck, screaming in Russian. Parker watched in his rearview mirror as Theo walked away from the roadblock.

"Good luck to you, too," Parker said quietly. He knew he had lost the best friend he had.

38

REESE NAVIGATED WHILE PARKER
drove.

"I think we're okay," she said, examining the map. "The problem is that this map is in Russian."

"I'm sort of surprised you can't read Russian," said Parker.

"Well, technically, I guess, you don't read Russian, you read Cyrillic. It's an alphabet that dates back to..." Reese knew she was giving Parker more information than he needed, so she stopped. "Anyway, I can't read it."

Parker grinned. "I knew I could find something you couldn't do if I hung out with you long enough."

Reese found herself blushing. The transmission made a horrible grinding sound as Parker shifted gears.

"Parker? Is something wrong with the truck?"

"It's not the truck. Fon-Rahm's spell is wearing off. Pretty soon I won't remember how to drive."

Reese was able to find the train yard, and Parker managed to drive there. They idled on a hill, looking down at the tracks, and they watched as men walked around the back end of an idling freight train.

"Are you sure we're in the right place?" asked Parker, absently playing with the dagger he had taken off the goon in the museum.

"They circled it on the map."

"I don't see them. Do you see them?"

"No, but the train's still here. Maybe they just haven't shown up yet." Reese put her feet on the dashboard, trying to get comfortable. Then she put them down again. "I don't know why you and Theo have to argue all the time," she said. "I would kill to have a cousin or a sister, somebody that has to hang out with me. I feel like I don't have anything in common with any of the girls at school. I guess maybe I'm not the easiest person to be friends with."

Parker seemed genuinely surprised. "Really? I think you're great. You're smart, you're cool. You're happy all the time. You're always excited by things. You're up for adventure."

Reese smiled to herself.

"If I was a girl, I would *absolutely* want to be your friend," said Parker.

Reese's face fell.

"There!" Parker sat up. Three Path members were climbing out of a Mercedes sedan. One of them carried Fon-Rahm's lamp. They all had guns.

"How are we supposed to get it back?" asked Reese.

Parker groped around the truck, never taking his eyes off the lamp. He came up with a dull green hat that he plopped on Reese's head and a ratty scarf that he wrapped around his own face.

"I'm going to drive down there and park right next to their car. You're going to sneak up next to the guy with the lamp and brain him with this." Parker pulled a massive wrench out from underneath the seat and put it next it to Reese.

"This," Reese said, "is a terrible plan."

"There are only three of them, and you know karate!"

"They have guns, Parker."

"We'll be out of there before they even know what happened! Just hit the guy and grab the lamp. I'll have the truck running right next to you."

Reese picked up the wrench. It was so heavy she could barely lift it.

Parker said, "Okay. I'm just going to creep down there real slow. They'll think we're army guys looking for something on the train. Are you ready?"

"No. I'm not doing this."

"Well, do you have any other ideas?"

"Yeah, my idea is we *don't* do your plan."

Parker moved around in his seat and accidentally hit the gearshift. The truck lurched forward and started to roll toward the train tracks.

"Uh-oh," he said, grinding the gears.

"Parker, stop the truck!"

"I'm trying! I don't know how to drive!"

The truck shot down the hill. The Path members dove out of the way right before Parker creamed the truck directly into the Mercedes. When they looked up from the crash, Parker and Reese found themselves once again surrounded by men with guns.

"I told you this was a terrible plan," said Reese.

One of the Path members ordered the others to board the train with the lamp. As they ran off, the leader grabbed Professor Ellison's bag from Reese and pushed Reese and Parker against a wall.

"Parker, I'm scared," said Reese. She was trembling.

The Path member checked his rifle.

Parker was in shock. Everything had gone so wrong, so fast. "This was all supposed to be fun. I just assumed it would all work out. I'm so sorry I dragged you into this, Reese. I really thought we could pull it off."

Parker wished that Fon-Rahm was there to save them, but he wasn't.

Reese took Parker's hand.

"Good-bye, Parker."

The Path member raised his rifle and took aim.

39

JUST AS THE PATH MEMBER PULLED
his trigger, the barrel of his gun bent upward, as if being pulled
by an invisible force. The minion looked at it, bewildered. It
was a good gun. Very reliable. The barrel had never turned to
rubber before.

He heard a voice say, "Hey, moron," and he turned around just
in time for Theo to crack him in the face with the giant wrench
from the truck.

"That's my cousin," Theo said.

Reese was pretty happy to see him. "Theo! How did you..."

Theo shook his head and pointed to his left. Maksimilian was
there, his hands raised to the sky. He was the one who cast the
spell that saved them.

"I'm a little rusty," Maks admitted, "but I still got it." Then he let out a burp.

"Gross," said Reese.

"The train!" said Parker. The train was moving, with the Path members and Fon-Rahm's lamp on board. Parker snatched Professor Ellison's bag off the ground and took off after it.

"Parker? Where are you going?" said Theo.

Parker was on the move. He thought he might be able to catch the train, but it was picking up speed and moving away from him fast. Parker slung the bag over his shoulder as he ran. He reached for the railing on the back of the train. He missed. He reached again and this time got hold of the railing by his fingertips. He tripped and was dragged along for a moment, but he managed to find his footing and, finally, pull himself on board the train. He tried the door that led into the train's last car. In his first burst of good luck all day, Parker found that it was unlocked.

40

THE TRAIN WAS OLD AND NOISY, AND it pitched from side to side as it sped down the tracks. Parker found himself in a freight car loaded with boxes and equipment piled high and strapped in place. He grabbed what he could to steady himself, and made his way carefully and quietly deeper into the train.

When he heard voices, Parker stopped and ducked behind a stack of crates. He peeked out. Two Path members were sitting on some gear, eating sandwiches and drinking coffee out of paper cups. One of the men had his hand on the glowing metal lamp.

Parker hunted through Professor Ellison's bag. He came up with a jeweled snowflake, which he thought didn't really fit the occasion, and a small porcelain ballerina doll, which he rejected as too girly. Then he found an amulet made of a piece of clear amber attached to a soft golden chain. He held the jewel up to the light. Inside the amber was a tiny, fossilized spider, trapped since prehistoric times in tree sap that later hardened into a gemstone. Parker felt a power flowing through the talisman. He knew instinctively that he didn't need any fancy spell to make the thing work. He just needed to point it and believe.

Parker aimed the amulet at the Path members. He felt the thing start to heat up. Before it could do whatever it was going to do, however, the train hit a stretch of uneven track. The car bumped and bounced, and the jewel went flying out of Parker's hand. It landed in the middle of the car, right where anybody could see it. Anybody, like, say, the thugs armed with machine guns seven feet away.

Parker froze, but the minions kept on eating. They didn't see it. One of them wadded up his coffee cup and threw it to the side. Then he got up and made his way to the front of the car. He slid open the car's huge side door, unzipped his pants, and started to, as Parker's dad would have said, make some yellow snow.

This was Parker's best shot. He grabbed the dagger from his waistband and cut the straps holding the pile of crates in place. Then he scratched the crates with the knife, making an unpleasant sound. The man with the lamp didn't hear it. Parker did it again, louder this time. The Path member grabbed his gun and got up to investigate. Parker waited for him to get close, and then he shoved. The crates fell on top of the minion, knocking him silly.

Parker was pleased with himself. All he had to do now was grab the lamp and set Fon-Rahm free. The second he reached for it, though, the other Path member came storming back, his gun at the ready. Parker had overestimated the amount of coffee the guy drank and how long it would take him to pee.

Parker pulled back his hand and threw himself behind a huge crate just as the goon started blasting with his machine gun. The box was marked in Russian and had a series of holes near the top. It smelled bad, too, but Parker didn't have time to complain. Bullets ripped through the car and knocked the lock off the big crate.

The lamp was just sitting there, right in the open. It was Parker's only chance. He waited for the Path member's ammo to run out. Then, when the minion stopped to reload, Parker jumped out and made a desperate grab at the lamp.

He came up about a foot short. The lamp was out of Parker's reach when the thug clicked the new magazine into place. Parker looked up to meet his doom, but a noise from the crate behind Parker startled him and the Path member. It was a growl, or maybe a roar. The gunman lowered his weapon and leaned forward, peering quizzically at the crate. Then the crate burst open and a polar bear meant for a circus in Poland, and upset at being woken from a deep sleep, leaped at the Path member. The goon screamed and tried to fight the bear off, but it was no use.

When the bear was through with the Path member, it turned to Parker. It didn't know what the metal container in Parker's hands was, and it didn't care. It had faced weapons before. Parker twisted the thing, and the bear found himself thrown back by a sudden explosion of smoke and lightning that cut the train car in half.

When the fog cleared, Fon-Rahm and Parker found themselves in the wreckage of what was once a train car. They were stopped on the tracks while the rest of the train chugged on, towing the other half of the freight car in a trail of sparks. The polar bear had had enough of people and lightning and trains. It was out of the car and running from the tracks on its way to a new life.

Parker scooped the amber amulet off the floor. You never know when something like that might come in handy.

"I missed you, buddy," he told Fon-Rahm.

"Yes," said the genie. "I suppose I missed you, too."

41

"THEY HAD ME OVER A BARREL,"
Maksimilian said. He was, along with Reese, Theo, and Parker,
trying to keep up with Fon-Rahm as the genie rushed through
the train yard, ripping open steel shipping containers. "The truth
is, I got soft. Pip-squeaks like the Path never would have gotten
to me a century ago."

Parker took off the professor's bag and handed it to Reese.
"Will you do me a favor and carry this purse?"

"Why?"

"It's a *purse*," he said.

"Who's going to see you?" Reese asked.

"Nobody. Just, please?"

Reese rolled her eyes and took the bag. Boys.

"When this one," said Maks, pointing to Theo, "came to

me for help, I just couldn't say no. It was a chance to wipe the slate clean and stick it to Nadir. He's a hard man to like. Plus, I couldn't very well pass up the chance to actually see one of the Jinn in action. Legendary."

Maksimilian stopped, winded. "That's enough for me. I believe there is a gallon of vodka with my name on it." He offered his hand to Fon-Rahm. The genie stopped tearing through the metal containers long enough to take it. "I can sense there is something big happening, but I'm in no shape to help. All I can do is wish you luck."

"I'll see you later, Maks," said Theo.

Maks winked at him. "Give my love to Julia. I'm sure she'll forgive me in a thousand years or so!"

Maksimilian walked away, his laughter echoing through the train yard. Fon-Rahm went back to his search.

"Maks is right. Something big is happening. An impending doom descends upon us, and Xaru is one step ahead. There will be a reckoning."

"Where?" Parker asked.

"Your home."

Reese said, "But our families, all our friends..."

"They are all in great danger."

"We have to get back," said Theo.

"How?" said Parker. "The jet's totaled and we're halfway around the world."

Finally, Fon-Rahm found what he was looking for. He tore the doors off a shipping container and stepped inside. When he came out, he unfurled an ornate carpet on the ground. Fon-Rahm looked at the kids and then back to the carpet.

"Not big enough," he said.

He went back to the container and unrolled a massive sheet of linoleum.

"You're kidding, right?" asked Reese.

"We have no time to lose. Climb on and sit down."

The kids stepped onto the center of the linoleum and sat. Fon-Rahm stepped to the front edge. Smoke misted from his eyes.

"You may want to hold on," he said as the linoleum rose into the air.

42

REESE'S MOTHER HAD READ HER
stories from *One Thousand and One Arabian Nights* when she was
a small girl. Reese had found the book too scary, but she did like
one thing: the flying carpet of Prince Houssain. When she was
tucked in bed, Reese had imagined herself flying on her own
magic carpet. She would go to London to see Mary Poppins and
drop by New York City to visit Eloise. She would fly across the
ocean, the wind blowing through her hair. She would smile and
wave at the people below, so far away they looked like ants.

Now that she was actually on a magic carpet (or a magic piece
of linoleum; really, it was pretty close), she had a completely different reaction. She was terrified.

"I'm going to fall off!" she screamed as the linoleum ripped
through the air.

"You will not fall off," said Fon-Rahm.

"How do you know?"

"Because I have made it so."

Reese trusted the genie. She locked her fingers on to the edge of the linoleum and carefully, carefully looked over the side. They were flying over the ocean at unimaginable speed, yet the wind was no worse than as if she were home riding her electric bike. They were so low that they were skimming the water, the linoleum tearing a white wake through the waves. Dolphins were chasing alongside. A whale breached not a hundred feet away.

All of Reese's fear was gone. She was mesmerized by actual, real-life, swear-to-God magic.

"When I was a kid I dreamed of flying," she said, "but this is better than anything I ever imagined."

"I think, you know, I might be sick," Theo said. He was still in the middle of the linoleum, trying his hardest not to yak.

Reese said, "Over the side, please."

Fon-Rahm strode to the front of the makeshift craft, where Parker was staring out toward the future.

"What if we don't get there in time?" Parker asked.

"Better to think of more pleasant things," said Fon-Rahm.

Parker turned to look at his two friends. He had come so far since his days in Los Angeles, and so much had happened. Maybe the most amazing development of all was his new friendships with Theo and Reese.

"Reese and Theo truly care about you." Fon-Rahm spoke as if he could read Parker's thoughts. "I know that it is hard for you to give your trust to anyone, but your new friends have earned it. Perhaps it is time for you to let them in."

"Theo gave up the lamps," Parker said.

"He made a mistake."

"What if he makes another one?"

"He will. As will Reese. As will you."

"But not you."

Fon-Rahm thought for a moment. "I was not sure that you would return for me or that you possessed the courage and the skill necessary to free me again. I underestimated you, and that was a mistake."

"Fon-Rahm, was that a compliment?" Parker looked surprised.

The genie allowed himself a grin. "Let us call it an observation."

"I've been thinking," said Parker, "about what's going to happen when we get home. There's going to be a fight."

"There is going to be a war."

"Then we should use every weapon we have."

"You have something in mind?"

"A little strategy and some insurance," said Parker.

The genie nodded. "We can discuss it on the way." He aimed the linoleum at the sky, and in seconds they were tens of thousands of feet above the sea, so high they could see the curve of the earth.

Fon-Rahm called out to Reese and Theo. "We'll be there in an hour or so. You will need your full strength. You should try to get some rest."

Reese stayed glued to the side, where she watched a 747 fly by underneath them. "That doesn't seem likely," she sighed.

43

PROFESSOR ELLISON HAD KNOWN PAIN.

She had almost drowned once, when her boat was sunk by pirates off the coast of ancient Egypt. She took a Spartan arrow to the shoulder in the Peloponnesian War. She twisted her ankle fleeing from Rome when the emperor Nero set the city on fire, she was tortured on the rack for weeks when she found herself on the wrong side of the Spanish Inquisition, and her hair was singed to a crisp when she was tied to a stake during a particularly nasty witch hunt in Scotland. An artillery shell shattered her leg near Verdun in World War I.

But the worst pain was the hunger she had felt when she was still a girl named Tarinn, poor and begging on the streets. She had gone days without food, and the pain in her empty stomach had been enough to double her over. A slumlord took "pity" on her and made her his property in exchange for a bowl of rice. She cleaned, she cooked, and she slaved. She accepted her regular beatings as part of the price she paid to keep the pain of starving at bay.

It was at the tables of the wealthy, serving food that she herself was forbidden to touch, that she first heard the stories of the dark sorcerer who bent the laws of nature to his own will. A man who could do magic, real magic! A man who never went hungry, who never had to bow to anyone! A man who had conquered pain!

Then she found Vesiroth, and for years, the pain went away. He didn't listen to her, but he didn't thrash her as long as she stayed out of the way, and eventually, grudgingly, he became her teacher.

She learned small things at first. How to read, how to pronounce the arcane language in the texts, how to cast a spell, how one spell combined with another. It was there that her thirst for knowledge of the Nexus became unquenchable. She was enthralled at the feet of her mentor. She learned how to sway emotions. She learned the secret to living for thousands of years.

She also learned a healthy distrust for the power that attracted her to Vesiroth in the first place. She was not surprised to find herself enchanted by him. He was a sorcerer, after all, and the passion that poured from the wizard with every breath was mesmerizing to his young apprentice. He was magnetic, and Tarinn could at times barely force herself to look away. But as she studied the books and legends, she found story after story of wizards who had destroyed themselves in the never-ending quest for power, and story after story of good intentions twisted by the accumulation of might. Power brought ego, and ego brought more ego, and she saw that it was all too easy for someone with a noble goal to become the very thing they hated most. A human being was just a human being, and human beings were creatures of fragile minds and hurt feelings. They lashed out when they felt threatened, and the more power they had, in Tarinn's experience, the more they felt attacked. People with power saw enemies everywhere.

Vesiroth had always been gruff. He had a frightening temper and was quick to lash out. He was also, even after his centuries of solitude and the immense knowledge he had acquired, human. There was a hurt that lay deep inside him and, horrible as it was, it kept him connected to the people he saw age and die all around him.

She could sense a change in Vesiroth after she brought back the last piece of the Elders' spell. When she read the spell on her own (not aloud, of course; she wasn't suicidal), she realized with a sudden certainty that if her mentor used it, he would be corrupted to his soul. The exposure to the power that was the Nexus would be too great. His mind would snap. The Elders knew the spell would bring only suffering. That was why it had been so hard to find.

Tarinn tried to bring Vesiroth back from the edge, but it was far too late. The Nexus called to him. The temptation of power was too strong.

She had to get away. Away from her mentor and away from the frightening power of his vengeance.

Away from the pain.

"This can all be over, witch. Release the spell and give me the lamps."

Xaru was inches away from Professor Ellison's face. She was in Yogoth's grip, his four arms holding her like a straitjacket. Her face was bruised, and she was experiencing the most intense pain of her long life. Xaru and the four members of the Path he had brought with him had not shown her any mercy. They were more than willing to kill her if it meant that they would take possession of the lamps. They were more than willing to kill her even if it didn't.

"No," she said.

They were in her office on the campus of Cahill University. All of her treasures, so carefully cataloged and arranged, were scattered on the floor. Shelves were tipped over. Her clippings were torn from the walls. They had found the shimmering wall, but none of them could breach the magic field she had placed to protect the only things she owned that could not be replaced.

"Don't be a fool, Tarinn. Give me the lamps. Spare yourself hours of torture."

"No."

The professor knew that it would be useless to scream out. There was no one there to help her. Fon–Rahm was buried under tons of rock. The children were probably dead. She was doomed. After thousands of years of life, she was finally going to see what came after.

Xaru grabbed her by the hair. "You are seconds away from becoming a limbless torso. Give me the lamps!"

The professor looked the genie right in the eye and spoke with steely conviction.

She told him, "The next time you see a lamp it will be from the inside, and I will be the one that put you there."

Xaru could take her impertinence no longer. His anger took control. His fist became a flame as he pulled it back to hit her and put a stop to her meddling once and for all. Professor Ellison closed her eyes, ready for the end.

Before the punch was unleashed, Nadir grabbed Xaru's arm.

Xaru paused for a brief moment. "Please," he said, his voice hiding his fury at Nadir. "Please tell me that you did not just grab my arm."

Nadir let go of Xaru's arm. He was calm as he bowed to his master. Then he turned to Professor Ellison. She tried to squirm away, but she was held tight by the drooling genie Yogoth. Nadir placed his hands on her temples and locked his scary blue eyes onto hers. His grip became tighter as his concentration grew more and more intense.

"No," she said. She was shaking, but not with fear or pain. She was shaking as if something were being pulled from her. "No. Stop."

Nadir doubled his efforts. He was reaching deep into her mind, probing her for the spell that would bring the lamps into the open. His hands trembled. His teeth clenched. Finally, the professor screamed and passed out cold in Yogoth's arms.

Nadir turned to the shimmering wall. Then he chanted a few words and reached in his hands. The wall parted at his touch, revealing four metal canisters floating unprotected in a sea of pure energy. Nadir smiled. The lamps were theirs.

44

THE CAMPUS WAS A GHOST TOWN.

That was the first thing Theo noticed when they landed. It was the middle of the day, on a Tuesday, and Cahill University should have been busy and noisy and crowded. There should have been a rush of students changing classes. There should have been professors drinking coffee and marking papers on benches. There should have been Frisbees. There should have been music. There should have been life.

There was nothing. All the students and the faculty and the workers were lying on the grass or on the sidewalks, motionless and silent. The only sound was the chirping of birds.

"We're too late," said Theo. "They're all dead."

Fon-Rahm shook his head. "No. They are not dead. Only sleeping."

Parker knelt by a collapsed student and put his fingers to his neck, looking for a pulse. "He's right. They're all unconscious."

"What happened here?" Reese asked. "It looks like they all just passed out at the same time."

"A trick of Xaru, no doubt. He does not like to be slowed down."

All of a sudden, Parker was frightened. He knew that Xaru was dangerous, but so far the only people that had gotten hurt were a few Path members. This was his first glimpse of what Xaru was capable of on a larger scale. If he could entrance an entire college full of people without breaking a sweat, what was to stop him from doing much, much worse? All the bodies on the ground could easily be dead, and instead of hundreds there could be thousands. Or millions.

"Dad!"

Parker looked up to see Theo running through the quad. Reese and Fon-Rahm were chasing after him.

Theo dropped to his knees. Both of his parents were sprawled unconscious on the sidewalk.

"Dad! Mom! Wake up!"

Theo was slapping his father in the face, trying to get him to snap out of his trance. Parker reached Theo and put his hand on his cousin's shoulder. "Theo. It's okay." Parker's voice trailed off. Lying next to his aunt Martha and uncle Kelsey was Parker's mother.

"Mom?" he said. He held her head in his hands and turned to Fon-Rahm and Reese. "She came! She came for Thanksgiving, and they were giving her a tour. She actually got here." He paused for a moment, and then screamed at Fon-Rahm. "Make her wake up! I command you to make her wake up!"

Fon-Rahm was stone-faced. "I cannot. The only way to wake these people is to stop Xaru."

Parker put a hand to his eyes so that no one could see that he was starting to cry. He pulled himself together and stood. Theo was lying on the ground, one arm around his father and one arm around his mother. Parker gently pulled him away.

"It's okay, Theo. We'll save them."

Theo, stunned, managed to stand.

"We got this," said Parker.

Fon-Rahm zeroed in on Professor Ellison's building. "They are in there."

Reese nodded. "Then let's go get them."

They ran through the archaeology building, down deserted hallways and past empty rooms. When they reached Professor Ellison's office, Fon-Rahm turned to the kids.

"I can take care of Xaru and Yogoth. You must deal with the Path on your own."

The kids nodded. They were outmanned and outgunned, but they knew they had no choice. They would do whatever it took to stop Xaru and the Path.

Fon-Rahm looked at them with something like respect. Then he turned the handle on Professor Ellison's office door, and the wall exploded in front of him.

45

AT FIRST, ALL THAT PARKER COULD see were bright white spots that danced in and out of his vision. As soon as he focused on one, it vanished. Parker couldn't tell if they were really there or not.

Soon, though, his head cleared enough to see what had happened. He had, along with Theo and Reese, been blown backward by an explosion. It didn't take long for Parker to realize what caused it.

"Now really, Fon-Rahm," said Xaru, hovering three feet off the ground in the ruins of Professor Ellison's office. "What took you so long?"

Xaru released a ball of flame that Fon-Rahm easily deflected.

"There is no reason for more innocents to be hurt. Surrender, Xaru!"

"Oh, I don't think so," said Xaru. He gestured to the back of what was left of the professor's office, where the Path members were just completing the ritual to open one of the newly freed lamps.

"No!" Fon-Rahm cried, just as the sacrificial Path member twisted the lamp. Fon-Rahm was too late. The lamp was open.

But nothing happened.

Parker helped Reese and Theo to their feet. They rushed to Fon-Rahm's side.

"Could it be a dud?" Parker asked.

"I fear not," said Fon-Rahm.

Nadir walked over to the kneeling Path member and casually slit the man's throat. The sacrifice slid to the floor without a sound. Nadir peered into the open canister. Then his face turned gray. He leaped for cover just as the lamp detonated, erupting with the fury of a blazing sun. Everyone in the room was tossed away from the blast.

Again, Parker found himself on his butt. He coughed and waved his hand in front of his face to clear away the smoke and dust. When he saw the sky he realized that the roof of the building was gone, obliterated in the explosion.

And then he saw Rath.

The newly freed genie was a horror. He was huge, the size of a building, so massive that he couldn't even fly. He had squirming, squealing rats for hair, attached to his horrifying head by their hairless tails. Any resemblance he had to Fon-Rahm, Xaru, Yogoth, or even Vesiroth was hard to see. He was simply a roaring monster.

Rath wielded two giant, curved scimitars and howled at the heavens.

"Oh, crap," Parker said. "You are a big boy, aren't you?"

The Path members were dumbstruck. They dropped the professor, who collapsed to the floor, and then they fell to their knees in front of the rat genie. Insane with rage that had been building for three millennia, Rath swiped with his twin swords, instantly killing the kneeling thugs. Only Nadir and one other Path member survived.

Fon-Rahm marshaled the kids behind him. "Take cover."

"What are you going to do?" asked Parker.

The genie took to the air.

"I'm going to keep them busy," he said as he flew off to do battle with Xaru, Yogoth, and Rath. The genies sized each other up. There was suddenly a lot of firepower in the airspace over Cahill University.

Reese was searching around the rubble.

Theo asked her, "What are you looking for?"

She pulled out the professor's bag. It was dusty, but intact. "This. There has to be something useful in here."

Parker saw Nadir and the remaining Path member coming for the unconscious professor. "Theo! Can you get to Professor Ellison?"

"Yes."

Parker took the bag and threw it to Theo. "Then take care of her. She's the only one who can trap the genies."

"Got it."

"Good," said Parker before he threw an age-old bowl from

the professor's collection that smashed against the remaining Path member's head, knocking him out cold. Nadir turned away from Professor Ellison, livid, and drew his curved blade. He was getting pretty tired of this meddling seventh grader.

Parker took Reese's hand. "We should probably go."

Reese nodded. "You're probably right."

Parker and Reese ran, with Nadir right behind them.

Fon-Rahm withstood the fire from Xaru, and he held his own against the mindless fists of Yogoth, but Rath was harder to ignore. His swords cut huge arcs through the air, and when one hit Fon-Rahm's arm, it cut him deeply. The wound would heal, but it would sap precious strength from Fon-Rahm just when he needed it most. They were going to wear him down. They were going to punish him for standing against them.

And they were going to enjoy every second of it.

Theo held Professor Ellison's head in his hands. At first he was afraid that the professor was dead. Her face was pale, and she felt almost weightless in his arms. For the first time, Theo saw Professor Ellison for what she was: a very frail, very elderly woman.

Then, with a start, the professor came to. Theo scooted away from her in fright. He rushed back when she made it clear that she was trying to stand.

"Don't try to get up, Professor."

"I have to," her voice was a hoarse croak. "I have to contain them."

"You're too weak!"

"Nonsense! I'm stronger than I have ever been!"

She got to her feet and raised her arms. Before she could cast any kind of a spell, she fell back into Theo's arms. He lowered her gently to the floor and bowed his head, wondering what they would do if she was too far gone.

Parker and Reese ran through the wreckage of the building.

"Do you think we lost him?" Parker asked, looking over his shoulder. A thrown dagger stuck angrily in the wall behind them.

"No," said Reese.

"This way!" Parker pulled Reese with him, but he was too far from Fon-Rahm. He broke down from the searing pain in his head.

"Parker! Get up!" Reese pulled him to his feet, but he could barely move. Nadir kept coming. They were not going to be able to run away.

The battle in the air shifted as Fon-Rahm clutched his head.

"Now! He's weakened!" said Xaru. Yogoth grabbed Fon-Rahm from behind and held him while Rath used his mammoth scimitars to slice hundreds of rats from his own head. Rath couldn't fly, but the rats could. They streamed at Fon-Rahm, their razor-edged teeth dripping venom.

"Now, this should be fun," said Xaru.

Reese saw that Fon-Rahm was struggling and in real trouble. She braced herself and did the last thing in the world that Nadir expected. She dropped Parker and charged him. Nadir made a quick stab with his blade, but with the skill of a martial artist, Reese planted one foot on the ruins of a wall and launched herself at him. His knife missed and Reese punched Nadir as hard as she could in the throat. Nadir went down, gasping for breath, and Reese picked up Parker. She dragged him back to the professor's office and he revived.

"What happened?" he asked.

"Nothing," she said. "Just giving Nadir something to remember me by."

With Parker close, Fon-Rahm recovered instantly. He threw off Yogoth and obliterated the attacking swarm of rats with a burst of blue lightning. Yogoth and Rath charged at him from opposite directions, enraged, but Fon-Rahm flew straight up and out of their way. The two brutish genies smacked into each other, and Fon-Rahm landed on top of them with enough force to leave them both dazed.

"Such heart!" said Xaru with a laugh. "I'll miss you when you're a pile of dust!"

He blasted Fon-Rahm with white-hot flame.

Parker and Reese knew they could only go so far before Parker's tether held them back, and now they were out of options. They were trapped.

Nadir turned the corner and saw them. He held his wounded throat as he walked slowly and deliberately, straight at them.

Parker pointed to the only way out. It was a hallway strewn with rubble. At the other end was a hole that led to the outside.

"Go that way," he said.

"No!"

"I'm the one he wants. Let him chase me."

"I'm not leaving you here alone! He'll kill you!"

"Reese. I have this covered. It'll be okay. I swear. Go."

Reese paused.

"I'll be okay. I promise," said Parker.

She nodded and turned to the hallway. Parker sprinted away and around a corner. Nadir, holding his throat with one hand and his knife with the other, went after him and out of sight. Reese tried to go the other way. She even started to. But in the end, she couldn't help herself. She turned on her heels and followed them.

Theo and Professor Ellison had great seats for the battle of the genies, but Theo would have rather been anyplace else. Even math class, Theo's least favorite thing in the world, was better than this. All he and the professor could do was watch as Fon-Rahm was worn down by the other three genies. Fon-Rahm was powerful, but he was also overmatched. He would block Rath, only to be sucker punched by Xaru or battered by the four fists of Yogoth.

Theo came to the only conclusion he could possibly reach. "Fon-Rahm can't beat them," he said. "He's just not strong enough."

The professor looked to her own useless hands and gritted her teeth.

Nadir was confused. He had followed Parker into a maze of destroyed offices, but somehow lost him among the debris. The Path leader had spent almost his entire life working to make Xaru's rule a reality, but at this moment, blinded by rage, the only thing he wanted was Parker's slow and painful death. Nadir was a man used to suppressing his emotions. He was violent and cruel, yes, but not because he enjoyed it. Everything he did was to advance a goal. This was different. Killing Parker was something he was actively looking forward to. Nadir had never before felt such hatred.

Where had the child gone? Nadir stepped into a destroyed classroom. Two of the walls were completely torn down. He kicked over a desk, expecting to find Parker hiding behind it, but there was nothing there. He huffed in exasperation.

"Looking for me?"

Nadir whirled on the voice behind him and was met with the hard edge of a Bronze Age shield in Parker's hand. It caught Nadir on the chin and knocked him sideways. Parker raised the shield to deliver a harder blow, but Nadir was a trained fighter with instincts to match. He grasped the shield and wrenched it away from the seventh grader. It clanged to the ground, out of the boy's reach.

Parker was defenseless, but not beaten. He charged at Nadir with his fists.

"Come on!" he cried. "Come on, you coward!"

Nadir slipped his punches with ease, and with one blow thrust his blade into Parker's chest.

Reese was watching from the doorway. "Parker?" she said, her hands over her mouth in horror. "Parker!"

Then Nadir pulled the knife from the boy's heart, and smiled as Parker Quarry slid to the floor, dead.

46

NADIR WIPED THE BLOOD FROM HIS blade on Parker's shirt. He had killed many, many men in his life, but this death was by far the sweetest. He would have liked to have savored it for a few moments more, but Reese was standing in the doorway, paralyzed with fear. There was no time for Nadir to contemplate his own successes. The girl needed to be tended to, as well.

He stepped over Parker's lifeless body and walked slowly at Reese. He wanted her to be good and scared when she died.

"Oh, I don't think so."

Nadir froze. He recognized the voice coming from one of the destroyed walls, but he knew that his ears were playing tricks on him. It was impossible.

He turned slowly and saw Parker step over the ruins of the wall and into the room. The seventh grader was with Reese and Theo, but that didn't seem right, either. Theo was with the professor in the other room, and Reese was still standing in the doorway. He could see her.

Nadir looked down at the boy he had just killed and saw that the body was dissolving into sand.

"Don't look so confused, buddy. You're not the only one who knows magic," said Parker, and Nadir knew. Doppelgängers! Magic doubles! Tricks, no doubt conjured up by that wretched witch who Xaru called Tarinn.

Nadir was enraged. He charged at Parker. Fine, he thought. Now I get to kill Parker Quarry twice.

As Nadir took his first lunging steps, Parker—the real Parker—aimed the amber charm from Professor Ellison's bag at him. Heat and vibrations come out of the amulet, and Parker could have sworn he saw the spider inside the amber twitch its legs. Then the jewel fired out a blinding yellow light that hit Nadir in mid-stride. As the magic struck him, Nadir began to rapidly age. His blond hair turned white and his skin wrinkled. His bones grew brittle and his head drooped. Only the hatred in his cold blue eyes remained intact.

Nadir's pace was slowed to a crawl, but he did not back down. He continued to come at Parker, deliberate step by deliberate step. By the time he reached Parker, Nadir was so old that he could no longer hold his knife. It dropped to the floor. With one final lunge at Parker, Nadir collapsed. He was now an old, old man, gasping for air and too weak to move.

Reese hated Nadir, but she couldn't bear watching years being taken away from anybody's life in seconds. "That was horrible," she said.

"I know," said Parker, taking her hand. "But right now we have to go." Reese nodded her head, and with one glance back over her shoulder at Nadir, she and Parker took the fake Reese and Theo and ran to rejoin the fight.

"It's the end for you, brother," said Xaru. Fon-Rahm was being battered by another onslaught of rats sliced from Rath's head. He was swatting them away, one by one, but their accumulated bites, added to the punishment from Yogoth's fists and the fire from Xaru, were taking a toll. Every time Fon-Rahm blocked one attack, two others struck him.

As Fon-Rahm evaded a swipe of Rath's swords, Xaru grabbed him and gave him a nasty head-butt to the face. "You should have joined me when you had the chance."

Professor Ellison had seen enough. She stood on shaky legs, brushing aside Theo's offer of help. "Give me my bag."

Theo did what he was told. Parker and Reese, with the fake Theo and Reese in tow, reached Theo and the professor just as Fon-Rahm kicked Rath through a wall.

"Where did these two come from?" Professor Ellison asked, nodding to the fakes as she searched inside her bag of tricks.

"I had Fon-Rahm summon them on the way here," said Parker.

"Smart," said the professor approvingly. "Maybe I can find something for them to do." She found what she was looking for, something in a soft velvet bag with a pull-string. "If I'm going to capture those genies, I'll have to prepare. Fon-Rahm will have to buy us some time."

Reese looked up at the battle. Rath had returned, hauling his bulk back into the building with a roar of anger. Fon-Rahm threw off Yogoth again. Xaru peppered Fon-Rahm with blasts of fire and laughter.

"That's not going to happen!" cried Reese. "He's getting killed up there!"

"That's true. But that would change if he had more power."

Theo said, "How can he get more power?"

The professor looked Theo dead in the eyes. "I can lend him some of mine," she said. "With your help."

"I can't help you! I don't know anything about magic or spells or any of this!"

"I would have preferred to bring you along more slowly, but we don't have the time and there's too much at stake. I need you to tap into your potential right now and help me."

Theo cast his eyes down. "I don't know how."

"You do; you just don't realize it yet."

Professor Ellison shook a glass prism from its velvet bag. "This spell is a doozy, and I'm too weak to cast it myself. I need you to concentrate on this prism and repeat the words I say. If I'm right about you, and I think I am, a good part of the power I have absorbed through the centuries will flow from me to you, and from you to Fon-Rahm. It's the only way."

"What if you're wrong about me? What if the thing on the plane was just a fluke?"

"Then we all die in an explosion of fire and ash. No pressure, Theo."

Theo didn't have a choice. He took the prism in his hand.

"Okay," he said. "I'm ready."

"You had better be," said Professor Ellison. She pushed Theo's hand up so the prism was between them and the genie fighting above them, and she began to chant words older than history.

Theo repeated the words. Even as the professor's voice wavered from her effort, he could feel raw power flowing through him. It was a strange sensation, like nothing he had ever experienced before. His hair stood out, as if someone was rubbing a balloon on his head, and he tasted metal. Finally, the spell was done, and the power left Theo in a burst of purple mist that enveloped Fon-Rahm.

Professor Ellison fell limp to the floor. Theo hoped against hope that whatever they had done together was enough to save all of their lives.

Fon-Rahm saw the mist close around him. He closed his eyes and took a deep breath, drawing the mist into himself and feeling the professor's years of accumulated power stream into his body. For a moment he thought the wreckage of the building that surrounded them was getting smaller. Then he realized that he was, in fact, growing larger. In seconds he was a giant, a colossus striding through Cahill University. He dwarfed even Rath.

Xaru paled as Fon-Rahm grew and grew. "What . . ."

Fon-Rahm flicked the attacking rats away with the tiniest movements of his fingers. He caught one of Rath's swords in each hand, tearing them away from the rat genie and casting them aside before crushing Yogoth beneath his titanic foot.

Xaru hit him with all of his might, but he barely felt it. Fon-Rahm pulled back his fist and let fly. He caught Xaru in the face and blasted him half a mile.

"You were saying?" he asked.

"You did it!" Reese told Professor Ellison. "He can win!"

"No," the professor said, struggling to her feet. "He has enough power to destroy the others now, but only *I* can trap them, and I only have enough strength left for one good try." She looked around the wreck that was her office. "Theo, all of you. Get me four containers. Jars, bottles, anything that can be sealed."

Parker raised his eyebrows. "Three," he said.

"What?"

"You said four containers. You meant three."

The professor smiled slyly, caught. "Of course. That's what I meant. Three."

With his new power, Fon-Rahm dominated the other genies. He was so huge and scary that Rath turned and lumbered away from the fight. Fon-Rahm grabbed Xaru by the throat. He held him and hit him again and again.

"You're time is up, Xaru. I'm sorry you could never listen to reason."

Xaru smiled through his pain. "That's always been your problem, big brother. You never learned that reason only goes so far. Now!" When Xaru yelled, Rath stopped stumbling and lashed out, not at Fon-Rahm, but at the kids and Professor Ellison. The rat genie knocked them aside and grabbed Parker.

Xaru laughed as Rath pulled Parker away from Fon-Rahm. "You never learned how to be truly vicious. You never learned how to do what it takes to win."

Fon-Rahm reached for Rath, but Yogoth held him back. Rath moved farther and farther away, straining the limits of the tether. Soon both Parker and Fon-Rahm were in searing pain. Parker felt sure his head would explode. He pressed his hands to his temples and screamed.

Xaru told Rath, "Not so quickly, my brother. Let's take a moment to really enjoy this." He floated lazily over to Fon-Rahm. "There's no escape for you this time, Fon-Rahm. This time *I* win. When the world is mine, do you think they'll remember you? Do you think they'll care whose side you were on? Now you have nothing, while every living thing on this world will pray for mercy in my name!"

Xaru slapped Fon-Rahm across the face. Fon-Rahm was helpless to stop him.

"All right, Rath," said Xaru. "We have much to do, and only eternity to do it in. Let's see what happens when we get these two a few miles apart."

Reese's stomach dropped. Parker was going to be killed. Fon-Rahm was going to be destroyed. Xaru was going to win.

47

REESE LOOKED OVER HER SHOULDER and saw herself.

"The doubles," she said. "We can send the doubles!" She grabbed the fake Reese and the fake Theo and yelled something in their ears. The doubles nodded and started to hunt through the professor's ruined gear.

"What can they do that we can't?" asked Theo as the fakes pulled a long orange extension cord from the debris. They each grabbed an end of the cord and ran at Rath.

"They can *die*," said Reese.

The doubles made a mad dash at Rath, winding underneath his legs in attempt to get the rat genie tangled up.

"That will never work," said Professor Ellison. "That thing is too big. Even if they manage to trip him, he'll still have Parker."

Reese told her, "I didn't tell them to trip him. I told them to make him mad."

Rath was, indeed, getting annoyed. He stomped at the fakes, but they were too fast. He couldn't pin either of them down.

"Ignore them!" commanded Xaru. "Finish the boy!"

Ignoring pests was not in Rath's nature. He kicked at the doubles, and then swung at them with the fists that held Parker. The rat genie was just too slow to make contact. Finally, enraged, he dropped Parker so that he could have full use of his hands. Rath balled up his fists, timed his blow, and crushed the fake Reese and the fake Theo into the ground. Satisfied, the genie lifted his fists. He seemed perplexed to find nothing but sand beneath him.

Theo and Reese were already dragging Parker back to be near Fon-Rahm.

"Are you okay?" said Reese.

"I got the wind knocked out of me."

"And your head almost exploded," said Theo.

"Yeah," Parker admitted. "There was that."

With his head recovered, Fon-Rahm was himself again. He rained blows on Rath and Yogoth until their fight was over, and then turned to Xaru. "It is over, Xaru. It is finally finished."

Xaru, exhausted and bloodied from the battle, took in the scene. His brother genies were spent and useless. The children were out of his reach. The professor was already lining up two old jars and a wine bottle, ready to trap him and the others. His fire, once stronger than a blowtorch, was dying.

"Go quietly," said Fon-Rahm. "Do not make me hurt you anymore."

The professor was ready to begin her chant.

"I won't be trapped again, brother," Xaru said.

"You made your decisions yourself, Xaru."

Xaru stared off into the distance. "There are things I know that you don't, Fon-Rahm. Things Vesiroth thought you would disapprove of. Things he thought you would not understand."

"Stop talking in circles."

"If I can't rule the world, no one can." Xaru closed his eyes and floated into the air. He raised his arms to his side and began to chant to himself.

Fon-Rahm was confused. "What is it? What is he doing?" he asked Professor Ellison.

"It's Vesiroth's spell of destruction. It was designed as a fail-safe, one last weapon that would destroy his enemies and leave him standing. I didn't think anyone else knew it. If Xaru finishes, everything surrounding this building will be vaporized."

Yogoth came out of his stupor and joined Xaru in the air.

The professor said, "Make that everything for miles."

Rath pulled himself up and joined his brothers from the ground. Lights started to flash around them.

Fon-Rahm launched a volley of lightning at the chanting genies, but Vesiroth's spell had created a shield around them. The lightning dissipated as it hit.

"I can't reach them through the shield," said Professor Ellison. "Can you bring it down?"

"No. It is too strong. The energy needed to breech will obliterate them as well." Fon-Rahm was stuck. "I cannot stop them without destroying them."

"You know that can't happen," said Professor Ellison.

"I may not have a choice."

The professor was using a Sharpie to draw arcane symbols of containment on her bottles and jars. "I just need a few more minutes."

"There is no time!" said Fon-Rahm. "If I do not stop Xaru now, he will finish his spell!"

"Let him finish, then!" Professor Ellison snapped. The kids were shocked. Ellison pushed Parker aside and spoke directly to Fon-Rahm. "You and I will survive!"

Fon-Rahm could hardly believe what he was hearing. "But the children, the town..."

"There are other children and other towns! There will always be more people. It will be easier to trap Xaru after he finishes the spell. He'll be tired. He'll be weak. Let him do what he wants."

The chanting from the genies was getting louder. Parker could feel the air around him changing. He knew the spell was almost complete.

"Fon-Rahm, don't listen to her!" he said. "I command you to destroy Xaru and protect us!"

Fon-Rahm hesitated.

"You can't do it, can you?" said the professor. "It's because you know I'm right. The greater good takes precedence over your master's whims. That's why you wouldn't obey Vesiroth in the first place. You know that if you destroy Xaru and the others, their power will return to Vesiroth and he will walk again. What is the sacrifice of one pitiful town and three children next to that? Let them die!"

Static electricity filled the air. Lights and smoke swirled around. The end was coming.

Fon-Rahm looked to the genies, and then to Parker.

"This is a decision I cannot make," he said. "You must command me."

48

ONLY WEEKS AGO, PARKER WOULD
have made the decision in an instant. He would have ordered
Fon-Rahm to annihilate the other genies, no matter what the
cost was to anybody else. Now he was torn. He wanted to save
himself and his friends and his mother, who was unconscious less
than five hundred yards away. He wanted to tell Fon-Rahm to
blast Xaru out of the sky, and deal with the consequences later.

But he wasn't sure.

What if he made the wrong decision and the world was con-
demned because of it? What if he unleashed Vesiroth and more
people died than would die here? The decision was too much for
any seventh grader, so Parker did what any seventh grader might
do. He turned to his friends.

"I don't know what to do," he said, looking to Theo and Reese. "This is bigger than just me. I need your help."

They stood in silence, thinking, for as long as they dared. They knew they didn't have much time.

"We have to let Professor Ellison trap them," said Reese. "We have to save the world, no matter what."

Parker nodded. "Theo?"

Theo said, "No! We can't! You heard the professor! Everything will be wiped out! My parents are here! Your *mother* is here!"

The lights spinning around them grew more intense by the second.

"They're almost finished!" said Professor Ellison.

"Parker, I don't want to die," said Theo.

Parker said, "I don't, either."

Theo, tortured, stared at the floor and nodded. Reese put her arms around him. Parker spoke up to the giant Fon-Rahm. "Let Xaru finish. Even if it means we're destroyed." He looked to his friends. "It's what we decided."

"You would make that sacrifice?" said Fon-Rahm.

Parker took Reese's hand. "We would."

Fon-Rahm nodded. "And that is why humanity deserves to make her own decisions."

With that, Fon-Rahm made the only choice that made any sense to him. He turned his immense power on Xaru and the other genies. Professor Ellison cried out, but he ignored her, concentrating all of his firepower on the shield. The shield buckled and fell, and the genies, powerless, were engulfed in Fon-Rahm's storm of lightning.

Xaru cackled as the Nexus took him. "You were always a fool, Fon-Rahm. This is only the beginning."

Xaru let out one final scream as he, Rath, and Yogoth were vaporized.

49

ALL WAS STILL.

Parker, Reese, and Theo stared at each other. Fon-Rahm knelt down so he could speak to them on their level.

"We're still alive," said Reese.

Parker said, "Why, Fon-Rahm? Why did you do it?"

Fon-Rahm had a gleam in his eye. "I do what I am compelled to do," he said.

Parker smiled at him, and the genie smiled back.

Theo was not interested in anything so touchy-feely. Reese had to hold him back from attacking Professor Ellison. "She would have killed us!" he screamed. "She wanted us dead!"

"Let her be," said Reese, staring daggers at the professor. "She never pretended to care about us."

The professor smirked. "Children. You think you know everything." She held out her prism and craned her neck to talk to Fon-Rahm. "I believe you have something that belongs to me."

"Yes. Yes, of course." Fon-Rahm placed his hand over the prism and closed his eyes. All the power the professor lent him returned to her in a purple fog, and Fon-Rahm shrank to his normal size.

"You should have kept it," said Theo. "It might've come in handy."

"It was never mine to keep."

Parker turned pale, remembering suddenly that his mother was still passed out on the grass. "My mom!"

He started to run out of the building, but Fon-Rahm grabbed him. "She is not hurt. Now that Xaru is gone, she and the others will awaken with no knowledge of what happened here."

"I have to see her!"

"Shouldn't we get our stories straight first?" asked Theo. "I mean, how are we going to explain all of this? We destroyed an entire building."

"I can just have Fon-Rahm put it back the way it was," Parker said.

Reese shook her head. "It won't last. In a day or two it'll be a pile of bricks again. And this time there might be people in it."

Professor Ellison took a step back and looked at what remained of her office. "It was an old building," she said. "And I often smelled gas. I believe that I put a few complaints in writing over the years."

Reese said, "Really?"

"No. But I'm sure I can whip up a convincing forgery or two." She looked at Parker and Theo. "You might as well run along to your parents. No one needs you here."

They didn't have to be told twice. Parker and Theo sprinted across the university campus, leaving Reese, the professor, and Fon-Rahm behind them.

All over Cahill University, students and faculty were waking up. They were groggy and confused, but they were safe and they were alive. An administrator found himself dangling halfway out of his Saab. At first he thought it was strange, but then he forgot all about it, the way you might forget an intense dream the second you wake up. A sophomore wondered in a vague way why she had decided to take a nap facedown in the middle of the quad instead of going to class, but the thought quickly vanished from her head, replaced by more pressing concerns like her GPA and the fact her roommate kept eating all of her ramen noodles no matter how many times she told her not to. A custodian was only slightly curious as to how it got so late. He would put off cleaning the men's locker room until tomorrow. There was plenty of time.

Theo found his parents on the sidewalk. His father weighed more than two hundred pounds, but Theo hauled him to his feet as if he were a small child. Theo's mother ran her fingers through Theo's hair, and he grinned like it was Christmas.

Parker's mother was coming to on the ground next to a bench. She blinked at the sun as if she had been asleep for weeks instead of hours. Parker wanted to run to her, but he stayed back. He didn't know what to feel.

Then his mom looked at him. She squinted as if she couldn't quite make him out.

"Parker?" she asked.

That was all it took. Parker ran to her and threw himself into her arms. He hugged her as if he hadn't seen her for three thousand years.

His mom hugged him back. "I missed you, too," she said. "I missed you so much."

Professor Ellison and Fon-Rahm watched respectfully, as far as the genie's tether would allow. The professor couldn't stop her eyes from misting over.

"Do not tell me you are going to cry," said Fon-Rahm.

She composed herself with a snort. "I haven't cried since Thomas Jefferson insulted my cooking."

Reese had gone back to the archaeology builing for one last look. She was out of breath when she caught up to them.

"Everyone from the Path is gone," she panted. "All of the bodies and everything. I couldn't even find Nadir. And there's something else. Your lamps are gone!"

Professor Ellison shrugged as if she had been expecting the news. "Well. I suppose I had better get back to work, then." She allowed herself another moment to watch Parker and Theo with their families. "Tell them I said good-bye, please. I'm sure I'll see them around." She turned back to her office and shouted over her shoulder to Fon-Rahm.

"Keep your eyes open. Things are about to get much, much worse."

50

THE MERRITT HOUSE WAS FILLED WITH people and the smell of roasting turkey on Thanksgiving. Uncle Kelsey sneaked a swipe of mashed potatoes before they were ready, and was rewarded with a playful slap from his wife. He was in a great mood. The explosion that destroyed most of the Cahill University Archeology building was chalked up to a gas main rupture, and just by sheer luck, not a single person had gotten hurt. Plus, some secret donor had already pledged enough funds to rebuild the entire structure. There were good people in the world. Reese helped Theo set the table in the other room. Her parents lounged in front of the TV, her dad happily watching football while her mother shook her head and wondered why anyone in their right mind would allow their kids to play a game in which somebody might be seriously hurt.

Parker's mom sat with a smile on her face, happy to be with her family and some new friends. Maybe today was the day that she would tell her son that she had decided to move to New Hampshire. Her original plan was to wait until Parker's dad was out of jail, but he was in for another year at least, and time was too precious to waste. Parker needed a family and, looking around, it seemed to her like he had one here. When he got out they could all move in together. She had already started looking for a job and a place where she and Parker could stay. It was going to be great, she thought, a new start for all of them. And New Hampshire seemed like the perfect place. It was so quiet and peaceful.

Parker stood outside and watched them all through a window. "My mom, Reese's folks, my aunt and uncle. They don't even know that anything happened. Everything seems like it's back to normal, but nothing will ever really be the same again, will it?"

"No," Fon-Rahm said from the shadows nearby.

"I wish my dad could be here."

"Is that a command?"

Parker thought for a moment. "No. I don't think I'm ready for that yet."

"Your mother cares very deeply for you. I would tell my mother how much she meant to me. If I had a mother."

Parker grinned. "You've got me."

"Yes," said the genie. "I suppose I do."

Parker's aunt yelled from inside the house. "Parker! We're eating!"

Parker said, "Let's go inside."

"Very well. I shall make myself unseen."

Before Fon-Rahm could make himself disappear, Parker stopped him. "Maybe we could try it another way," he said.

They were all sitting patiently at the table when Parker came in with Fon-Rahm. At first, Reese and Theo were confused. Why was the genie wearing Dockers and a button-down plaid shirt? The Fon-Rahm they knew was a magical being that performed miracles with a wave of his hand, not a schlub in a cubicle on casual Friday. The bigger issue for the kids, though, was that everyone in the room was looking right at him. Was it possible that they all could . . . see him?

"Mom, everybody," said Parker. "This is Mr. Rommy. He's our new math teacher at school. I hope you guys don't mind I invited him. It's just that he didn't have any family around to spend Thanksgiving with."

"Oh, it's our pleasure," said Aunt Martha. "It's so nice to have you." She was already back in the kitchen for another plate.

Uncle Kelsey pulled another chair up to the table. "Any friend of Parker's."

Fon-Rahm sat in between Reese and Mrs. Quarry. Reese smiled warmly at the genie. She thought she saw him blush.

"Mr. Rommy, is it?" asked Reese's mother. "That's an unusual name."

"It's very old," he told her. "I believe in the beginning it was . . ."

Theo and Reese held their breaths, hoping he didn't start talking about ancient Mesopotamia.

"French," said Fon-Rahm. The kids relaxed.

Parker's mom said, "Well, I'm thrilled that Parker has someone to look up to. I'm almost afraid to ask you how he's doing in your class."

Fon-Rahm sized Parker up. "Parker," he said, "is an excellent student."

Parker beamed.

His mom was pleasantly surprised. "Good! That's good to hear!"

Parker took the seat next to his mom. "This is great, Mom. I'm really . . ." He gave her a genuine smile. "I'm glad you're here."

She took his hand on the table. "Thank you, Parker." She thought she might cry, so she turned her attention back to Parker's new math teacher. "I hope you're hungry, Mr. Rommy."

"I am. Do you have any French fries?"

"Try the mashed potatoes," said Parker.

They all dug in, thankful for many, many reasons.

After dinner, as the adults drank coffee and digested their turkey, Parker, Reese, Theo, and Fon-Rahm stood in the backyard and stared up at the night sky.

"I never really appreciated the stars before I almost got killed a bunch of times," said Theo.

Fon-Rahm said, "You know, it might not be such a bad idea for me to come and teach at your school."

"Excuse me?" said Parker.

"That way we could remain within the tether's limits and we would be ready if we were needed."

"I'm not crazy about this plan."

"Oh, I think you will find that as a teacher I am tough, but fair."

"The whole point of having a genie is to avoid things that are tough but fair."

Fon-Rahm was thoughtful. "I wonder if they would give me my own parking space?"

"Do you really think that Vesiroth will come back, after all these years?" Reese asked Fon-Rahm.

He looked to the moon. "I do not know. It has been a long time, and he has only regained three small parts of his power. It would be difficult, I think, for anyone to endure what he was put through."

Reese was relieved.

"Of course," Fon-Rahm continued, "Vesiroth is the most powerful sorcerer the world has ever known. If anyone could have survived all this time, it would be him. If he has revived, his anger will know no bounds. Even in a weakened state he poses a dire threat. And let us not forget that there are still nine more of the Jinn out there, somewhere."

Fon-Rahm saw that he had worried Reese.

"No," he said, shaking his head. "We will never see Vesiroth. His body was probably destroyed years ago."

"Good," said Parker. "I think we could all use a little downtime."

EPILOGUE

THE CARNIVAL WORKER WALKED WITH a slight limp. He wished that he could say it was from getting bucked off a horse, or maybe that it was an old football injury. It wasn't. His leg just bothered him, that's all. The fact was, he was getting old.

"Now, see, when the ride jams, nine times out of ten it's right here," he said, pointing his flashlight down. "The track is bent."

His trainee furrowed his brow and nodded, all business. That was good, the carny thought. You didn't keep something like the Train of Terror running without knowing your stuff. It was an old ride, built in the sixties and showing her age. The carny could relate.

"I keep asking for replacement parts, but the owners are too cheap. Ah, what do they care about an old ride? I think I'm the only one who'll even notice when it finally stops running."

He had no idea how long that might be, but when it did happen, he knew he was probably out of a job. He had been touring with the carnival for more than forty years, and he had seen it go straight downhill. When he started, the rides were shiny and new. Now, the whole place gave off an air of seediness and disrepair. He wasn't even sure it was worth anyone's time to train the new kid. Still, the trainee wasn't so bad. He wasn't a genius, but if he was, he wouldn't have been there, would he?

It was dark inside the ride, and it smelled like stagnant water and metal. It was supposed to be a train through a haunted mine. The walls were fixed up to look like black rock, but the paint had fallen away in places, and the white stucco underneath poked through. The plastic skeleton on the first turn was missing a foot, and the thing that popped out from behind the dynamite kegs looked more like a mangy dog than a werewolf. Really, what was a werewolf doing in a haunted mine, anyway? A ghost would have made more sense. The carny guessed that it was too late to change it now.

As the carny bent down to look at the tracks, the trainee let out a yelp. He had backed into an iron cage hanging from the ceiling.

"Oh," said the carny. "Have you met Harold?"

The carny aimed his light at the cage. Inside was a mannequin dressed in rags and coated with shiny lacquer and a thick layer of dust. It was in a standing position, with one hand extended, as if he was reaching for something, maybe. The carny let the trainee stare at it for a few moments.

"It's a real body, you know," said the carny slyly.

"Get out of here."

"I swear. It's an Egyptian mummy. It was part of some old traveling exhibit. After they went bust, this thing ended up in here. They call him Harold because, well, I don't know why they call him Harold. He looks like a Harold." He lowered his voice to a whisper. "They say if you're in here by yourself after midnight, you can hear him moving around in there. One time, when I had just started working here, I heard him say something."

The trainee was skeptical. "Yeah? What did he say?"

The carny brought his voice even lower, making the kid lean in to hear him. "He said . . ." Then the carny yelled as loud as he could, "Lemme out!"

The trainee jumped and the old man laughed. "I'm just pulling your leg, you dope. Come on, let's go."

They walked down the tracks and out the exit. The carnival was closed. Workers swept the grounds and closed up booths.

"Ah, man," said the trainee, "I left my crowbar back there."

"Well, you had better go and get it. The last thing we want is for a car to derail because you left something on the tracks."

The trainee jogged back into the murky tunnel. He found the dent in the track and saw his crowbar on the floor. As he reached for it, his flashlight found Harold. The trainee stood up and peeked into the cage for a closer look. It sure was an ugly thing. Harold's face had been painted over so many times it hardly even looked like a face anymore.

The trainee smirked. A real mummy, right. And he was going to play shortstop for the Detroit Tigers next year.

He bent back down to get his crowbar. When the trainee stood, Harold reached out of the cage and grabbed him by his throat.

As he choked the trainee to death, the mannequin's lacquered mask crumbled away. Underneath was a face brutally scarred on one side. It was good to be free, thought Vesiroth as his lips twisted into a grim smile.